REBEL MOON

PART TWO – THE SCARGIVER

V. CASTRO

TITAN BOOKS

Rebel Moon Part Two – The Scargiver: The Official Novelization
Print edition ISBN: 9781803367330
E-book edition ISBN: 9781803367347

Published by Titan Books
A division of Titan Publishing Group Ltd
144 Southwark Street, London SE1 0UP
www.titanbooks.com

First edition: June 2024
10 9 8 7 6 5 4 3 2 1

A CIP catalogue record for this title is available from
the British Library.

Printed and bound in the United States.

ᚠ

NOBLE'S EYES WERE WILD WITH DELIRIOUS FURY. THE MEDICAL TECH'S GAZE
darted towards Noble and back to the hologram readout.
"Look at his vitals, I don't dare up the dosage."

"Do it!" said Dr Mons.

With hesitant steps, the assistant walked to the bio
mainframe and pulled a lever attached to a unit containing
different fluids. Through a clear tube, a viscous pale-yellow
concoction of sedatives traveled from the mainframe
into Noble's body. The room of techs watched on
silent tenterhooks.

Noble's entire body fell limp in an instant as the
sedation hit his system. The hologram displaying his vitals
showed his brain activity and heart returning to stable
levels. The new assistant closed his eyes and exhaled. The
rest of the techs went back to their previous tasks. Dr Mons
turned his attention to the assistant. "Now that he is stable,
we must continue to phase two."

A chrysalis of thin fibrous strings began to web across Noble's body. Every inch became covered in the membrane. The main doors to the medical bay opened. Cassius entered, his eyes immediately gravitating towards Noble. He watched in his usual stoic manner as his superior was being attended to. He moved to Dr Mons's side. "He's alive."

Dr Mons nodded his head. "He is… just." Cassius and the doctor watched Noble disappear beneath the slimy, tight casing.

"Have all the files pertaining to these procedures been sent to the Motherworld?" asked Cassius.

Dr Mons turned to face him. "Once we brought him back… we received a communique from the Motherworld with a list of bio-enhancements…" He walked towards the bio mainframe with multiple monitors. Cassius followed him and noticed the techs trying not to glance at Cassius, who would be in charge if any of this went wrong.

Dr Mons pointed to one of the screens. "I thought it was a mistake. We were lucky he was alive at all. No way he could survive the trauma associated with changing his biology on a molecular level. I protested and was told… 'If he dies, he dies.' I don't know who he angered at home, but this order came from the highest levels."

Cassius's eyes darted from scanning the document from the Motherworld back to the doctor. "Yet, he survived." He then glanced back at Noble. He wondered if he had sided with the wrong admiral. Was his loyalty misplaced with the wrong man? One thing he did know: if Noble wronged or challenged Balisarius, they would both be considered expendable. Perhaps another plan, in place for himself, would have to be conceived.

"Yes… he did. I don't know whose bad side he is on, but this order came from the highest levels. It is not for me to question," said Dr Mons.

"Call me when he is ready."

The doctor nodded and Cassius returned to commanding the ship.

Cassius walked closer to Noble just as his eyes began to flutter. He smacked his lips. The casing around his face and neck had already been removed. He winced as he swallowed hard. His eyes opened to narrow slits before squinting at Cassius. He opened his mouth to speak but no words emerged. Cassius turned to Dr Mons, who nodded. Cassius leaned his ear closer to Noble's lips.

"…Cassius. Cassius, where am I?" he whispered in a hoarse voice.

Cassius moved away from Noble. "You're aboard your ship, sir, *The King's Gaze*. We have been holding in orbit around Gondival hoping for your recovery, sir. And thank God our prayers have been answered."

Noble stared at Cassius. "If I had died, the ship would have been yours, Cassius."

Cassius did not respond or show the slightest emotion. It might have been his, but there would have been a lot to answer for to the Motherworld. "Sir... I'm just happy you're alive and we eagerly await your return to command."

Noble's eyes searched the room before meeting Cassius's gaze again. "Is that so... Well then Cassius, listen to me... Veldt. She's on Veldt," he said in a whisper through clenched teeth.

Cassius's brow furrowed. He had an inkling, but had learned long ago to let Noble lead. Sometimes it was better to act like you knew nothing to get precisely the information you wanted. "Who is?"

Noble attempted to lift his head and his eyes narrowed again, this time with an angry glare. "The Scargiver. The hated other. She's on Veldt. Set a course for Veldt."

"What about Devra Bloodaxe? The mission is not complete. I know we will be asked about the rebels and we need a satisfactory answer."

"Secondary. They are weak on their own. She won't stand a chance now. And when I have Arthelais in my grasp... No one will care she hasn't been captured yet."

Noble shook his head and blinked before he fell back on the platform. He stared at the ceiling without saying another word.

Cassius gave him a salute. "Yes, Admiral. It will be done."

He turned to the doctor and gave him a short nod, then walked back to the main deck to set their course and ensure their plan on Veldt was still in place. Before beginning his transmission to Veldt, while straightening his uniform, an officer paused the comms to start the hologram. "Do you think it's wise to tell them we are still on course?"

Cassius pushed the officer's hand away from the hologram pad, and made a point to keep eye contact. "We need the girl, and we need the harvest. Both await us on Veldt. No matter what fight they offer, both will be taken."

The officer saluted Cassius and left. Cassius paused in front of the hologram. For the first time, he felt his loyalty to Noble waver. He knew exactly who Noble was and what motivated him. It had taken years for him to know how to handle that man. But if Noble went down, then so would Cassius. He could see this had become personal. That was usually when matters became reckless and messy. He had seen many in the Imperium rise then fall because they became too willing to think they were above their station by taking liberties.

Balisarius made Noble seem like a wet nurse. Noble was not someone he was willing to die for. And these rebels made him pause. He'd watched them fight against great odds on Gondival. Two separate groups of rebels joined for one cause, to attempt to stand against the Imperium. The plan was meant to be perfect, yet Noble found himself defeated, and only one Bloodaxe was dead. They had proved they were willing to die for a united cause, and each other. This bond was greater than the Imperium, and that was dangerous.

KORA AND THE BAND OF WEARY BUT UNSCATHED WARRIORS MADE THE EASY journey from the lush forested mountains and into the tucked-away valley towards the village. Kora and Gunnar glanced at each other when they reached the edge of the dirt road leading into the outskirts of the village. They expected it to be bustling in activity, but it was the opposite. The village was quiet, seemingly desolate. No one worked in the fields or outside. All the uraki had to be in the stables because they too were absent. Kora turned to Gunnar with one hand on her hip, close to her weapon. Her body and face straightened with tension upon this odd sight. She shifted from calm and relief from making it back in one piece after fighting Noble to high alert. In a way, she was more comfortable in this tense state. "No one is in the fields."

Gunnar shook his head and scanned the village, paying attention to every detail. "Look. Smoke from the longhouse. The hearths are lit. Let's find out what's going on."

Gunnar and Kora picked up their pace towards the stone bridge as they approached the longhouse, hoping to find out where everyone was. As they got closer, Den and Hagen stood next to the village bell. Den had his eyes only on Kora, giving her a welcoming smile while Hagen waved them over. Gunnar glanced over to Kora, who seemed to relax upon seeing familiar faces. Hagen had a wide grin as he studied the warriors individually. They stopped at the posts to dismount and tie up the uraki.

"We watched your descent down the eastern slope. I am Hagen." His eyes softened as he said this and looked at Kora with genuine joy. Hagen approached the warriors with Den next to him. "This is Den. We welcome you to our humble village. You must be tired and hungry."

Titus held up his flask. "And thirsty."

Hagen nodded and clapped his hands together. "We have prepared food and drink for you in the longhouse." Gunnar slapped Hagen on the shoulder with a large smile then turned to the warriors. "Come on, you'll see what great hosts my people can be."

Hagen, Gunnar, and Den turned to walk into the longhouse. The rest of the warriors followed, with Kora staying behind the crowd. "Kora!" a voice shouted.

Kora saw Sam and smiled. She appeared well. The young woman waved to her then turned to run in the direction of the granary. Kora's gaze moved to the towering mountains. It was nice to feel rooted to the ground again in a place of such beauty. She inhaled deeply before turning to join the rest in the longhouse.

Sam ran into the granary, out of breath and rosy cheeked. "They've come back!" She stood in front of him, smiling and buzzing with excitement.

Aris rose from the barrel he sat on, fixing and cleaning weapons. This news made him equally excited. "How do they look?"

"Strong. I guess how warriors should look. I *knew* Kora would make it back. We have real fighters joining us."

Aris's initial excitement died down when he thought about the practical. "How many of them?"

"Six… with Kora and Gunnar."

He shook his head, appearing crushed by the number, and looked around the granary that still stored Imperium equipment. "Six? Then it won't matter how strong they look."

Sam's face dropped. "Oh."

Aris walked towards Sam and reached for both her hands when a series of loud beeps rang out. It was his superiors reaching out via the comms link. His eyes darted around frantically. "Hide! You can't be seen."

Sam nodded and ducked behind stacked crates. Satisfied she was out of sight, he rushed to the hologram. Before answering, he ran his fingers through his hair and made sure his uniform appeared tidy. He swiped the plate to receive the transmission. A familiar face appeared. "Commander Cassius," said Aris as he saluted.

"Soldier. All is as it should be, I trust?"

"Yes, sir. All is on target."

Cassius never surprised Aris with how difficult he was to read. The man was a master at never betraying his thoughts or emotions. He stared at Aris with a short pause. "Nothing out of the ordinary?"

Aris matched his stoic expression. "No, sir."

"Very well. Ensure the harvest is brought in as planned and ready for our arrival in five days' time." Cassius ended the transmission abruptly after saying this.

Aris stared at the space which Cassius just inhabited then slowly turned towards Sam's hiding space. "You can come out now."

Sam rose to her feet with caution. Her face no longer showed disappointment. There was worry mixed with terror at the memory of the violence they had experienced at the hands of the soldiers. Her voice warbled. "Five days?"

Aris nodded, looking just as somber. "We need to go to the longhouse now."

The longhouse was empty when the group of warriors entered. Only a single hearth had been lit, but there were loaves of bread, hard cheeses, dried fruit, fresh vegetables, and meat. Apples in a basket sat next to jugs of water and ale. Tarak turned to Titus after not seeing the villagers.

"Not much of a first impression… or welcome," he said in a low voice.

Hagen cleared his throat and clasped his hands in front the warriors. "Our villagers have prepared a bounty of food and drink to demonstrate their fealty and gratitude at your arrival."

Kora looked around the longhouse in confusion. "But where are they? Are they hiding?"

Hagen shook his head. "Not hiding themselves… To show their deference they hide their shame."

"Shame? Of what?" said Kora.

Den looked at Kora then back to the warriors. "How would you feel, the lot of you, if you could not stand for yourselves to protect your own home? If you had to ask others to lay down their lives for you? This has never happened in our history."

"Give them time. It's a difficult thing these people have done. To swallow their pride enough to even ask for help. That is bravery itself," said Milius, who then turned to Hagen. "They should see there is no shame in our being here."

Kora smiled at Milius then glanced back to Den and Hagen. "And as it happens, nobody need lay down their lives. A defense is no longer needed. Admiral Noble is dead. We killed him."

"*You* killed him, Kora," said Gunnar with eyes shining brightly as he looked at her.

Hagen appeared shocked upon hearing this news. He exchanged an excited look with Den. Both men beamed with large smiles. "You do not believe they will return?" asked Hagen.

"I don't. It's Imperial protocol, in the event of an admiral's death, to return to the Motherworld at once," said Kora, matching Hagen's joy. The room lightened as she delivered this news. Hagen stepped closer to her. "Then I owe you an even deeper debt than I..."

"You're wrong." Everyone turned towards the voice coming from the entrance of the longhouse. It was Aris with Sam by his side. He continued, "I've just heard word they will be here in five days."

Den's head snapped towards Kora. "I thought you said you'd killed Admiral Noble."

Kora's eyes searched the floor as she thought back to those final moments looking at his crushed body. The blood surrounding him like a red aura of death. "I did kill him. His body was smashed on the rocks. He is dead. It's against protocol to come without an admiral to command the ship."

Titus took a step forward. "We all saw him, but believe me when I say death is not always a deterrent for the designs of the Motherworld. They must be in more need of this grain than we could have known." He turned to Hagen. "Call your villagers."

Hagen gave him a nod before rushing out the door. Moments later, the loud clear tone of the bell rang through the village for all to hear. The group of warriors followed Kora walking out of the longhouse to join Hagen. The

villagers began to emerge from their houses, knowing the

bell was not a sound to ignore. They glanced at Hagen, then kept their eyes on the foreign warriors while keeping a respectful distance. When everyone seemed to be gathered, he addressed the crowd like the natural leader he was, standing tall with confidence. His deep voice boomed and carried.

"Dark days lie ahead of us all. When the time comes we may all have to stand together. In battle, as brothers, where no one life is more valuable than the other. To succeed, there must be trust between us. But trust is a river that must flow both ways. In time we will show you how to fight. First, we must see your strength and the way of the land. If we do not act quickly, the destruction of your village is all but assured." He paused to scan the crowd's reaction then turned to Hagen. "How long does it take to bring in your crop?"

"Half a cycle around Mara."

Titus shook his head. "It must be done in three days' time." Den and Hagen exchanged glances. There was a murmur amongst the villagers after he said this. Titus continued. "We need every man and woman who is able. The grain is the most powerful weapon. Without it they are liable to blow us out of existence from orbit. If we bring it in fast, we can use it as a bartering tool and shield."

Den turned to Kora. "I thought you said they wouldn't negotiate."

"Admiral Noble wouldn't have. The fact they are coming without him… Whoever is his second in command just might be willing to do a trade."

The villagers looked at each other with worry and skepticism. Some whispered to each other. No one else spoke out loud. Titus walked down the steps towards the villagers. "Rest well. The work begins at dawn." The crowd dispersed back to their homes.

Tarak moved towards the doors of the longhouse. "I am all for an early night, but can we eat now?"

Hagen nodded and extended his hand. "Please do, and use the longhouse as you wish. There are blankets and all you need to sleep here tonight. If you need anything, I am at your disposal."

Gunnar stepped closer to Hagen. "Why don't you also rest. I'll take it from here." Hagen nodded and left the warriors at the longhouse. Late afternoon drifted into dusk. They ate in silence: their first real meal on the ground, not packaged shit on Kai's ship that wouldn't spoil for a hundred years. Milius hung their head and looked at the fire in the hearth before raising their goblet of ale. "For Darrian. May he rest in power. And for Devra, wherever she is. May the winds of rebellion guide her where she needs to be."

"I'll drink to that," said Titus, gulping the rest of his ale before pouring another. There was no noise coming from the village except the calls of the uraki and Tarak taking big bites into an apple. Nemesis finished her food and rested on a mat on the floor. Kora took slow bites, still turning over in her mind what the Imperium could be planning with their break in protocol. When the sky became completely dark, Tarak turned the ale jug upside down. Not a drop slipped out. "Guess this means time to turn in."

Kora rose from her seat. "Probably a good idea." The others unpacked the bedding brought into the longhouse for them to sleep on. "I'll walk with you… I'm on the way," said Gunnar.

"Suit yourself."

THE EVENING ILLUMINATION FROM MARA SET THE FIELDS AND VILLAGE ALIGHT
with a celestial orange glow. A light breeze blew across
the golden fields. The villagers had lit the lanterns
hanging from their houses, drawing out the insects
that chirped in the warm light. Kora and Gunnar
walked at a languid pace towards the home she shared
with Hagen.

"Do you think they'll learn to trust one another? I
thought the village would be excited to see our return,"
said Gunnar.

Kora looked at the path ahead as she spoke. "They're
frightened. Of outsiders, of fighting an uncertain battle,
for their lives. Trust? I don't know. I just hope they have
the courage to stand and fight if it comes to that."

"I had no idea what it would be like to fight. And how
much it would scare me."

Gunnar and Kora stopped in front of her home. She

turned to face him. "You were afraid to die. It's okay. Everyone is."

He stepped closer to her. Close enough to see the reflection of the low lantern light in her eyes. "No. I didn't even think about dying in the moment. If you had asked me before how I'd feel, I would've said I'd be petrified. And I was scared, the most afraid I'd ever been in my life. But not of dying."

Kora held his gaze. "So what was it you were so afraid of, if it wasn't death?"

Gunnar remained silent, looking into her eyes, searching for the right way to say what he felt. "It was you… It was losing you."

Kora opened her mouth to speak, but she couldn't find the words to react to this revelation, the tenderness in his honesty and vulnerability in that moment. She stepped closer to him and kissed him. He pulled her to his body by her hips and kissed her back with heated urgency as their tongues slipped in and out of each other's mouths. She pulled away. "Wait."

"I'm sorry. I didn't…" said Gunnar with worry in his eyes.

"Don't be… just not here." She touched his chest. "Take me to your bed."

Gunnar caressed her cheek. His eyes blazed with an intensity Kora hadn't seen before. "Whatever you want."

Once behind the closed doors of Gunnar's house they fell into each other's arms. Their secret passion for each other could now be fully unleashed. Kora lay on his bed, with Gunnar following her. She pulled her thin top over her head. She wanted to feel his skin on hers. Their bodies glowed in the firelight as they kissed each other with a slow sensuality. Savoring the taste. She cradled his face to pull him closer to her. This moment turned to a hunger that needed to be satiated from the inside. And it wasn't just her body she wanted to give to him, it was also everything else.

His lips and tongue moved lower to tease her breasts. She unclipped and removed her bra to allow him to have more of her. She moaned softly with her eyes closed, as his hands massaged her breasts, as he kissed her nipples. Her body relaxed into sexual bliss as she allowed him to take his time exploring her body. His mouth moved towards her belly, where her scar could be seen and touched. Still he moved lower where she was as hot as the fire that heats the room.

Her back arched with the ecstasy only his lips and mouth between her legs could incite. She writhed without care to the movement of his tongue. Gunnar could explore her body in ways she wouldn't allow Den. Her thighs became wet and slick from his stimulation, as she sunk deeper into the abyss of lust, perhaps love. All that existed was the pleasure Gunnar gave to her effortlessly as she gave herself the freedom to receive and enjoy.

He moved back towards her for another kiss, his hand cradling hers. His emotions were no longer hidden as he touched her face with a smile. The hardness of battle and Gondival seemed a lifetime away in that moment of fire, breath and skin. She touched his hand tenderly and gazed into his eyes as he kissed her again. She wanted more and twisted her body to move onto her belly. His hands slid across her body as he remained behind her.

She cried out as he entered her from behind, their bodies melting into each other, rocking in sync with every thrust. Kora reared her head back, kissing him with feral abandon. He steadied his body with one arm while cradling her with the other, thrusting harder and deeper, like their kissing. She moved to her back so she could face him again with her legs spread. She rested her legs against his thighs as they continued to make love.

He lifted her up into the lotus position, still inside of her. Kora straddled him as he sat upright. Face to face, she ground her hips. Both moaned as they gazed into each other's eyes. His arms were around her waist as she cradled his head. His pleasure was giving her pleasure as he watched and felt how her body reacted whilst riding him harder. He steadied himself by leaning back into the bed as she continued to take the lead until she kissed him again and their arms found each other. Exhausted, they fell into the bed.

They lay in bed in each other's arms. His hands caressed her bare skin and she touched the hair on his chest. "What Noble said about you being the most wanted criminal in the known universe… You don't become that simply by running away."

She gave his chest a light kiss and paused before speaking. "I told you how I was raised by Balisarius, Regent of the Imperium. And that I was the bodyguard to the Princess Issa."

"Yes. That you were a decorated warrior and friend to the royal family. What happened to them?"

"Under the healing influence of his daughter, the king had begun to see many things in a different light. Word had reached him that his most celebrated general fought without honor, and that his main weapons were slaughter and cruelty. And so the king knew he must not let him retain his command. He should have destroyed Balisarius, and then me along with him... but the king loved him, and even through his rage saw him as a son. And so for his sins, he was made a senator."

Kora kneeled in the opulent and vast throne room. The heat shining through the colossal stained-glass window behind the thrones made her feel hot in her uniform. The rays were intensified by the moment. She lifted her chin and stared at the image on the glass. The great warrior queen of long ago—Issa's namesake—seemed to stare back. A large wolfhound stood next to her. The light filtered through her image like a holy warmth. For a moment she felt safe looking at those painted benevolent eyes until she shuddered with fear. The king's shouts at Balisarius shook her to her core. All she could do was kneel and remain silent. She had grown accustomed to orders. She didn't dare look at Balisarius or interrupt.

"What have you done? What have you done?! I trusted you! I gave you everything," shouted the king, who leaned forward in his throne. His face and neck appeared red from his anger. "When I was told you were a fraud and a liar, I defended you. And like a fool I defend you still. And yet you betray me, with each act of dishonor you slap my face, you spit on my trust, my loyalty, my faith. I loved you like a son, and like a son I gave you everything. But can a king love a butcher? I think not. And that is what you are… a butcher. Now leave my sight whilst I decide what to do."

When the king finished speaking, she looked up to see as much hurt as there was rage in the king's face. Guards moved to stand next to Balisarius and Kora. She stood and allowed herself to be escorted out of the throne room. Balisarius did the same, except there was no hurt in his eyes. He had a look of disgust. The large doors of the throne room shut behind them with an echoing bang, leaving them alone. Kora moved towards Balisarius. He snapped his head towards her, giving her a daggered look. "Not now." His eyes narrowed before storming off.

Kora didn't know what to do or where to go. She returned to her room feeling like her world might come to another abrupt end. If the king banished them, she didn't know what other type of life there could be for her. This was all she knew and Balisarius was her only family.

Kora kept her distance and remained silent, knowing the precarious ground she tread on with Balisarius. She was only part of the royal court because of him. Not long after, he called for her to meet him at his villa. She always knew the king was merciful. Instead of banishing or executing them, Balisarius was stripped of his military duties and placed in the Senate. Kora continued on in her usual duties. Her nervousness kept her awake the night before; the morning as she traveled to see him, her entire body felt tense, just like the first time she stood on a warship waiting for the doors to open to face an enemy. She didn't know what to expect after his cold treatment the last time they saw each other outside of the throne room.

He met her on the steps of his home with a wide smile. Something had changed: perhaps he had had a private meeting with the king. He opened his arms to embrace her. "Thank you for coming. I know you are busy with your duties."

"I am always happy to answer your call."

"Good. Let us have tea."

They walked into the villa and into the main sitting room on the left. There were only paintings of him in various suits of armor in different war campaigns. "Please sit, Kora," he said as he poured them both a cup of tea. She didn't like the smell and never drank it. But she would today. "Thank you."

"I would like to invite you the Senate for a special session. You can see firsthand what our future holds."

She took a sip of the hot tea and managed a smile. "I'm glad you are enjoying your new position."

"I think I may be able to do more here than in war. You wait and see. Next week all you have to do is arrive promptly."

"I will. Thank you for the invitation." Kora finished her tea without him asking how she had been or how she felt. But she excused it as him being preoccupied with his new position.

On the day of the visit to the Senate, Kora stood at the very back with the other non-senators only allowed in by special invitation. Balisarius stood with his eyes blazing with the intensity of a battlefield. His silence held the audience captive before his voice exploded with passion.

"With my own eyes, I have seen the horrors and degradations far from our own. Day in and day out I strode into battle on those worlds expecting a bullet to find my head or heart, caring not. I would give my life a thousand times for our most sacred Mother. I know that I would, for I made it time and time again, for that is what it means to be a true soldier. Yes, my days on the battlefield may be behind me, but I would still give my life, nay my very soul, to protect our world from the darkness that creeps in from the outer worlds. And it does creep towards us. I have seen it. We cannot lower our guard, we must raise it as we continue into an uncertain future, in the name of those before, and those after."

Kora was mesmerized by his vigor, as he pounded on the lectern, and his ability to speak eloquently while also knowing what to highlight with every inflection. For all his ferociousness on the battlefield, it was nothing compared to his skill and cunning as a politician, and in the echoing marble halls of the Senate did he find his true calling.

The entire room erupted into cheers. His face beamed as he watched them stand—for him. She glanced over to the king and queen, who neither applauded or smiled. They had a look of worry as they scanned the Senate's reaction. The princess was not there because she was still a child. Kora felt conflicted. She was from one of the "outer worlds", but her loyalty was to Balisarius and the king.

After the Senate session, there was a reception at the palace gardens. Spring brought the gardens to life with every blossom in full bloom and their scent filling the atmosphere. The sun felt warm without the harshness of summer heat. Violas played beneath a tent. Kora and Balisarius strolled towards a queue of politicians and foreign delegates waiting to meet the king, queen, and princess Issa.

"You did well today, Balisarius. Congratulations," Kora said. His face was stoic before he glanced around their immediate vicinity. Most of the guests spoke amongst themselves or had drinks in their hands.

He spoke in a hushed tone, but kept his calm as if all was well. "Daughter. The news is dire. I have learned the king plans to abdicate and pass the kingdom to the princess. He also plans to disband the empire. He said Issa had looked into his eyes and forgiven him. But now he must make things right."

His face twisted in disgust. "Can you believe that… *She* forgave *him*? I have never heard of such nonsense. A daughter should know her place."

That last sentence pinched something inside of her. "If what you say is true, Issa will rule with wisdom and reason. All the time I spent with her gives me that hope."

His expression hardened to a glare colder than the frozen lake at the winter palace when he looked into her eyes. "That all may be true, but when the cleansing begins, you and I would be the first to go. Everything we sacrificed for will be for nothing. We can't allow that. The Realm is more than you or I, or some little girl, and it won't be sacrificed by the guilt of a spineless king who, instead of ruling in his bloodstained chamber, hides behind the innocence of a child." The rage he felt was palpable. Kora glanced around, wondering if others noticed or heard. They still smiled and mingled in oblivion. No one else seemed to possess the same rancor.

"What can we do? It is the king's wish."

His eyes remained hard as he watched the crowds fawn over the royal family, but his lips curled to a sneer. "The king is just a man. Every general and half the Senate have their positions because of me." He looked into her eyes. "When I am Regent Militarium, you won't be a servant to the princess. You will take her place."

A shiver ran the length of her spine as the ice in his words covered her mind and thoughts.

"Senator, may I speak with you?"

He turned from Kora. "Ahh yes, Senator. We have much to discuss."

Balisarius left. She stood alone, trying to process his words. The brightness of the sun and music irritated her senses. As she scanned the crowd, looking for a way out, she locked eyes with Issa. The princess gave her a warm smile. Kora managed to return the gesture, but felt like a fraud. Her heart and loyalty divided. She touched her weapon, engraved with *My Life For Hers*, and prayed she would never have to choose.

Just as Balisarius had told her, the king made it known he would pass his responsibilities to his only child, Issa. The first event would be held on the newest and final Dreadnought. Both Balisarius and Kora would be present.

The yet-to-be-completed Dreadnought hovered above the clouds of the Motherworld, still attached to a construction platform. This was meant to be a moment that would change the course of history for the Realm. It was the dedication of what would be the last Dreadnought-class battleship. A symbolic end to an age of expansion started by her father and that would now be ended by his daughter in her first official act as leader. Before her coronation she would dedicate the ship's power source as was dictated by tradition.

For the secret to the Motherworld's domination across the universe was an inexhaustible source of energy derived from an enslaved creature called a Kali. At the core of every Dreadnought, these ancient female humanoids were kept in a half-conscious state, their bodies hardwired to the ship to drain them of their massive energy, fed on the organic matter of conquered worlds. And each blessed by a culpable king. And now this child would be the last.

REBEL MOON

33

Unimaginable distances and worlds became within reach. Piles of matter from destroyed worlds lay in heaps in the boiler rooms of the Dreadnoughts. In the heat, soldiers shoveled it into furnaces that traveled through pipes and fed directly into the bound Kalies' open mouths. In giant metal casings the same shape as their body, with their eyes half open, they stared into the mysterious void of space and time. In their state of half consciousness, they fed and bled energy to fuel war.

The royal dropship docked with the unfinished Dreadnought. The king, queen, and princess Issa disembarked. The young princess greeted Kora and an elite delegation of generals in a dusty rose pink dress and white gloves. Kora bowed her head and the generals did the same. "It is an honor to escort you to the engine room."

"Thank you, Arthelais." The princess appeared calm and poised with such a momentous occasion about to occur. The generals turned on their heels and the entire party followed Kora down a low-lit hallway. Only the light hum of the Dreadnought beginning to funnel power could be heard. They walked deeper towards the center until they could see Balisarius standing at the end of the hallway. He gave them a large smile upon seeing them. He held out his hands in welcome before kneeling. Kora didn't like this pretense. He had made it very clear previously how he felt about the princess.

"Princess."

She looked down at Balisarius. "You may rise, Senator. I'm not queen yet. But I can assure you that when I am,

I will decommission every Dreadnought and set *all* the Kalies free."

Because Kora knew him as well as she did, she could see the contempt he harbored behind his forced smile as he looked up at her. He rose to his feet.

"I would expect nothing less when you become queen. And on that day, I will give my life to defend whatever order you in your wisdom would choose to decree. But 'til then, I would only hope you respect your father and the Realm and fulfill your duty this day."

Princess Issa and Balisarius held each other's gaze as if locked in a battle of wills. Neither blinked, neither showing real warmth or betraying their true feelings towards each other. The hallway seemed to close in as everyone had eyes on the two individuals who could not be more different. She gave him a nod but did not speak. Balisarius returned the gesture and moved towards the king. "My liege, when the music begins, you and the queen will enter first, followed by the princess, giving her the proper symbolism. Then she will dedicate the Kali by opening the main power valve and pulling the veil from her plaque. The generals and senators will bow, completing the ceremony."

The king placed a hand on his shoulder. His eyes possessed a kind fondness. "I am proud of you. I thought you would have a hard time with this transition, but I see you understand the world must evolve, we must evolve."

Balisarius' lips stretched to a smile. "I do, my king… I do. I'll go in and check everything is ready."

"Thank you, Balisarius. We have had our disagreements; however, that has come to an end too."

Balisarius paused as he absorbed the king's words and presence. His expression softened into a brief but ineffable moment of sadness before he snapped back to his previous demeanor. "Wait for the music." His eyes glanced towards Princess Issa before he pressed the keypad to enter the darkened engine room. It automatically shut behind him.

The king crooked his arm for the queen to enter the room with him. They both gave Princess Issa warm smiles, their eyes shining with pride. The princess paused, her eyes roving around the hall before giving them a forced smile, then shifted her eyes towards the door with a nervous glance. The queen noticed her daughter's hesitation. "It's alright, darling. You only have to do this once and there is nothing to fear."

Kora stood back trying to remember the faces of her own parents, but her mind was blank. It didn't matter anyway. The silence of the moment was broken by the sound of string instruments. The low vibrato was the signal for them to enter. The door opened and the king and queen walked through first, followed by Princess Issa, then Kora, behind at the respectful distance. The musicians wore black sacks over their heads. In the center, there was a large open eye with a single tear. The room went silent as they entered. The king looked around in confusion. Before him stood a group of senators and generals. The king scanned the room and raised a hand to the air. He took three steps and touched a pipe. "These boilers are cold. And where is the Kali?"

Balisarius stood in silence next to the musicians. His face had the appearance of metal and malice, a chiaroscuro of deceit. The king and queen turned to see the senators walking towards them with unsheathed blades in their hands. The king whipped his head towards Balisarius, who also had a blade in his hand. The light reflected its sharpness. They locked eyes. Any emotion the king had for Balisarius was as cold as the boilers. "She warned me about you," said the king.

Balisarius said nothing. He looked towards Princess Issa, who had terror in her eyes as she tried to back out of the room, but the door was blocked by the generals. His hand tightened around the blade he lifted higher.

"Wait! No!" the king shouted to him. "She is only a child."

Balisarius looked at the king with eyes devoid of any humanity. Every moment they had shared together meant nothing to the traitorous senator who only had one care in the universe—his own glory. The king's face dropped knowing this was truly the end. He reached for the queen's hand when the generals set upon them and began to gouge them to death. The king attempted to shield the queen from the blows, but it only sped his own demise. Her strangled screams echoed through the boiler room, as did the king's shouts for help.

A general yanked her limp arm away from the king, who was on his hands and knees trying to speak. Only hoarse croaks escaped as he held a bleeding gash on his neck. His robes were soaked with blood. The queen tried to reach for him when the general wrapped an arm around her waist and slit her throat from ear to ear in front of the king. The deep gash went through her throat to her spine. Any further would have decapitated her.

Tears welled in his widened eyes as her body fell to the ground in front of him. Her head flopped back and dead eyes stared back at the king. Balisarius placed his boot on the back of the king's neck before lifting it up again and bringing it down until a snap could be heard. The king lay face down with eyes wide open next to his wife. Balisarius sniggered. "I am not the death of you or your bloodline. Your stupidity is."

Princess Issa whimpered as she stared at the bodies of her dead parents. She turned to Kora, who had taken off her leather glove and drawn her weapon with a trembling hand. It pointed directly at Issa. The two held each other's gaze. Princess Issa looked at the gun then back into Kora's eyes.

"Do it! Do it now! It is us or them," snarled Balisarius with blood spatter on his face and spittle at the corner of his mouth.

Princess Issa didn't look in his direction or at anyone else in the room. Her fate was sealed. Calm surrender crossed her tear-streaked face. "I forgive you," she said to Kora.

Kora's hand still quaked. She knew she had to do this, but didn't anticipate how difficult it would be to do.

She trusted her adoptive father. Sweat dripped from her temples. "Don't…"

"Kill her!" screamed Balisarius.

Kora's lips parted as she sucked in a breath of stale air smelling of copper, before pulling the trigger. Issa reached for her chest. The gaping hole released a bright light. The blinding flash caused Kora to wince and shield her eyes for a moment. She looked back to see the princess lifeless on the ground.

Memories of the princess as a young child flashed in Kora's mind. The life-giving light from her hands, her laughter, the walks with the king. Kora looked back to Balisarius. His face was a puddle of blood and tears. "What have you done?"

His eyes strayed from Kora to the generals who had just committed murder. They stared at her, still clutching their blades. Like a well-rehearsed symphony, they each called out, "Betrayer! Assassin! Murderer!"

She shook her head with pleading eyes. She looked back to Balisarius for reassurance or answers, anything to explain this. He slowly lifted his finger like a dagger. "There she is… the murderer of the royal family. An 'off-worlder', a cancer of ethnic impurity. The very thing we must fight! Seize her."

The generals moved towards her. Kora continued to shake her head. "No," she whispered with her weapon raised towards Balisarius. She couldn't pull the trigger. Her eyes scanned the dead bodies and pools of blood of those who had trusted her. Her heart exploded in that moment with a sorrow and bitterness she only felt when she saw her own dead family. The day she met Balisarius. And now he had betrayed her in the most evil, vile way she could imagine. To use her love and trust for his own gain and make her a sacrifice.

She clenched her jaw before pointing her weapon directly at the murderous general. One clear shot struck him straight through the forehead. Blood and brains sprayed the approaching traitor generals. She aimed at another and hit him in the left eye. He screamed as he clutched his face. The door behind her opened. Kora could hear the footfalls of soldiers: one crossed the threshold. As they began to enter the engine room, she didn't hesitate to shoot each one in turn while dodging their bullets. Her mind raced as she tried to comprehend the situation.

She backed away from the generals and soldiers whilst still shooting to clear her way. Just behind her, she could access an elevator to take her to the dropships and shuttles. She sprinted to the elevator and slapped the keypad.

Before she could enter, a bullet grazed her left arm. She screamed out before turning towards a soldier barreling towards her. As she raised her pistol, he swiped her in the ribs with the butt of his gun.

The blow sucked the wind out of her chest. She fell to the ground, hitting the back of her head against the cold floor. Her ears rang from the impact as she lay there stunned. He kicked her in the same spot. As he leaned down to lift her up, she managed a kick to his groin. His body curled forward. Kora lifted herself high enough to aim her gun and shoot him in the belly. With a bleeding arm, a throbbing ribcage and head, she entered the lift.

She had to get into a dropship. It was the only way out. She held onto the wall of the lift until it stopped and the doors opened. She jogged to the nearest ship and entered. Her fuzzy head scanned the bridge computer. She didn't know where she was going. The ship roared to life and jetted out of the Dreadnought. Kora leaned back into the seat on the control deck. Her entire body radiated pain, but it didn't come near to the pain of this betrayal. Now she was truly alone in this universe. She didn't care if she lived or died. Fate would make the decision in the end.

Kora lay in Gunnar's arms after she told him her tale. She loved the feeling of his chest rising and falling. The sound of his heartbeat. He remained silent. She propped her herself up with one arm. She searched his face for a hint of what he might be thinking. "I fought my way to the shuttle and have been living life as an outlaw ever since. That's me. The heart of my fall from grace and how I eventually found myself on Veldt."

He touched her cheek and moved strands of hair from her face. Before speaking he gave her a tender kiss on the lips. "I see now why you lied to Titus. He never needs to know the truth. I don't know what he would do if he knew the truth. I don't know what he would do if he knew what part you played."

Gunnar's warmth and understanding embraced her like his body. The love he exuded made her feel safe. He was a safe place to fall into, something no lover before him had given her. "It was all I knew. I thought about letting them kill me or just not fighting. But somehow the last words of the child... her forgiveness... I felt the only way to honor her was to run. To try to be... I don't know. More than a weapon."

He kissed her on the lips again. "You are. You are much more than that to me and the people here. Definitely to Hagen. What he went through seeing his wife and daughter's health deteriorate. Life can be cruel and unsettling."

She smiled. "More than a weapon. It's what we are all trying to be."

THE KING'S GAZE MOVED WITH SPEED AND STEALTH THROUGH THE CONSTANT midnight of deep space. The great void that belonged to no one, but for the Imperium, it waited to be conquered. Cassius stood in the conning tower watching their progress towards Veldt. It would end in one of two ways. Noble getting them all killed either through a battle, from the hand of the Motherworld, or total destruction of their target. No middle ground. Ever. Noble learned that after a disastrous first campaign straight out of the Academy. Cassius wasn't with him, but he heard about it. If Atticus were not from a military family from Moa, he would have never come back from that. He seemed to be able to come back from anything.

"Commander, I have the chief medical technician."

Cassius looked at the communications officer to his left. "Put him through."

The communications officer swiped the control panel.

The room filled with clashing shouts and curses. Cassius immediately recognized one of the voices.

The medical technician spoke. "Commander, I think you should…"

Before Cassius could speak, he could hear Noble screaming. "Get your hands off me! I have a ship to command, and no, I won't calm down!"

"You just need to come down here now," said the medical technician in an agitated tone.

The communications officer looked at Cassius then snapped his eyes back to the control panel when Cassius glared at him. "On my way."

The line went dead. Cassius inhaled a deep breath before leaving the command deck to see Noble. He walked swiftly to the medical bay, ignoring those who passed and saluted. He hated this feeling of babysitting, of managing someone who could cost him his life. When he entered the medical bay, Noble was stood next to his bed, arranging a crisp white sheet around his body in the fashion of robes despite the fact his entire body was still attached to the ceiling that connected to the medical mainframe. All he needed were laurels on his head—something he desperately wanted. He often thought Noble and Balisarius were cut from the same cloth.

"Sir, you're… you're awake," Cassius said.

Noble's face twisted with an incredulous sneer. "Of course I'm awake. Now tell this idiot to unplug me. That's an order." His eyes shifted to a medical tech closest to him.
Noble ripped a monitor electrode off his chest.

The tech stammered behind his mask, "Sir, there are protocols before you can be cleared to resume your command. Tests that need to be conducted to ensure you are mentally and physically strong enough to…"

Noble backhanded the tech across the face before grabbing him by the neck and squeezing. With one arm he lifted the tech off his feet. He kicked his dangling feet. The cruelty in Noble's eyes glowed. "Let me help you with the evaluation."

Noble tossed the tech across the room with clenched teeth. His chest rose and fell with his rapid breathing. The tech lay on the ground, coughing and rubbing his neck. Two others ran to his aid. Noble looked back to Cassius. "Do I seem strong enough to you, Cassius?"

Cassius recognized that wild glint in his eyes, along with something more sinister. He hadn't made it this far under Noble's command without knowing what battles to fight. He glanced towards the stunned medical staff. "Help him! Unhook him now."

The medical staff scrambled towards Noble, who had his arms outstretched, ready to be free from the black cables like a rabid dog waiting to be unleashed. Cables were unplugged with the skin carefully placed over the openings. One tech worked with diligence, carefully extracting the cable attached to Noble's head. He smoothed the skin over the ports to hide the seams that would stitch together on their own. When free from the cables, Noble glared at the techs scurrying away from him. He turned his attention back to Cassius.

"How far from Veldt are we?"

"A few days, sir."

Noble's attention seemed to stray as his eyes appeared as if they were seeing something only he could perceive. His head tilted towards the ceiling. His eyes scurried across the lights embedded in the ceiling. He lifted his hands and shifted his gaze to his fingers. They moved slowly before he made two fists. The veins in his forearms bulged and his muscles tensed. One hand moved to his chest. He ran his fingertips across the rough, puckered skin that created a crude scar on his sternum. He closed his eyes and squeezed them as if he was reliving the moment it had been created by that bitch Kora. His lips pursed and formed a tight straight line.

"Admiral, my apologies for the scar that was left by this incompetent medical team. I'm sure it can be removed."

His eyes snapped open. "No. Leave it. She gave it to me and when I deliver her to Balisarius and her body is displayed in the rotunda of the senate, I will bare my chest and this scar will stand as a symbol, that it was I who brought to justice the Scargiver. And it is *I* who stands before my people as savior."

Noble no longer looked at Cassius. His eyes and thoughts were far off, seeing his victory in conquest. Cassius wondered if this was the beginning of Noble wanting to challenge the authority of Balisarius. If so, they were entering dangerous territory. The Regent made it very clear who his enemies and allies were.

. . .

The sky over Veldt was illuminated with an indigo and yellow predawn glow tinged with Mara's red. A few stars and the moons were visible. Hagen entered the longhouse and banged on a small bell. The warriors sleeping on the floor sat up, bleary-eyed at the intrusive noise. One of the villagers brought in clothing and boots for farm work. No one complained, knowing what was at stake.

When the warriors were dressed and outside, Hagen stood on the back of the flat bed of a wagon ready to address everyone. The warriors and villagers stood in front of him, still waking up, waiting to hear the plan before time ran out. He searched the crowd with his eyes before he stopped and followed Gunnar and Kora approaching together. Den stared at them hard, his face crestfallen as he looked back towards Hagen's feet on the wagon. Tarak glanced back before doing a double-take. Kora and Gunnar attempting to avoid eye contact with anyone made it obvious they were uncomfortable showing up together so early in the morning with their clothes hastily put on— and by the looks of it, not rested. Tarak gave her a large grin and elbowed Titus.

"Sorry we're late," said Gunnar as he moved closer to Hagen.

Kora remained back with the warriors. Titus and Tarak continued to glance her way. She looked straight ahead. "Say nothing."

The two men giggled like schoolboys. "What? I can't say good morning?" said Tarak.

Gunnar stood next to Hagen and Den, who shot him a stoic glare before crossing his arms. Gunnar gave him a half smile, but wouldn't meet his gaze. He cleared his throat before turning to the crowd. "Let's begin. We have a few people here with us who have probably never harvested grain, made sheaves, or worked a scythe. But we will welcome them and, through our work together, win favor with the spirit of the soil and guarantee the future abundance of these sacred fields. You all know your jobs. Don't be afraid to personally approach our guests and put them to work."

A group of older women with their hair tied back, wearing loose trousers and long-sleeved blouses, approached Titus and Tarak. The leader stood in front of Tarak. She had silver hair with pale yellow streaks. Her light skin showed her age around her eyes and mouth, with creases like tilled rows in a field. Yet, her eyes sparkled with youthful energy.

"You two will come with me. We will follow the reapers and bundle the grain into sheaves. Do you think you can handle that?" Her gaze followed his chiseled shape, mostly his bare arms.

He looked at all the women who remained stony-faced and tanned from outdoor work. Tarak furrowed his brow and scoffed, "This sounds like women's work."

She flashed him a confident smile only a woman of a certain age and life experience could give a man. Hervor was a woman who didn't suffer fools because she had heard and seen it all before. "It is. That's why it might be too

much for you."

Tarak looked at her, stunned, his lips parted. Titus laughed out loud. "Lady, you already know him so well."

"We should get started before the sun is too high in the sky. Follow me." She turned to move with the other women by her side. Titus and Tarak followed in silence.

By the time the sun had risen above the mountains, everyone was hard at work. The rhythmic swinging of scythes in the hands of the reapers led by Den moved horizontally across the fields. Step by step, they worked their way through the tall golden stalks. Behind them, Tarak and Titus followed the lead of Hervor and her band of women. They gathered the fallen stalks into bundles and tied them together before leaving them in a pile. Kora, Gunnar and the rest of the warriors followed behind them, propping the bundles up against each other in the shape of a pyramid so they could dry. Hervor stopped her own work to help Tarak keep the stalks in a tight bundle between his thighs to tie it properly. She shook her head and smiled at him while showing him again the technique that required the strength of one's entire body. He smiled back at her as she moved.

Kora, who was not far behind, watched their interaction—which bordered on flirting. She chuckled and glanced towards Gunnar next to her. He also laughed, noticing the two, then moved closer to Kora. "He was chained up a long time."

"As a prince I assume he is used to having a lot of female attention, just not in this way."

Gunnar waited a beat. His expression became more serious. "You okay with… what happened last night?"

She glanced around to see who might be listening to their conversation. "Of course. But it's no one else's business."

"I know, but the way Den looked at me… It's not a secret how he feels about you, or his intentions given the chance."

"Well, just because we want something doesn't mean we get it."

"Gotcha."

"If I wanted Den then I would have been with him last night," Kora said without looking at Gunnar, continuing with her work. He paused for a moment to watch the way her body moved in the light.

Nemesis nudged him. "Love alone won't harvest this field, just like love alone won't save us from the Imperium." Gunnar snapped out of his reverie. Nemesis was already moving on. He took a deep breath and continued to lift stalks.

By late morning, everyone in the fields was ready for a much-needed rest. Sam and Hagen ensured there was enough water on hand. Nemesis wandered through the field, away from the small talk. In both hands she carried smooth wooden threshing sticks. A light breeze caressed her skin and blew strands of thin black hair from her face. She closed her eyes and stood in a wide stance, allowing the elements to guide her mind and body. With sticks in hand, she raised her arms from her sides and allowed the wind to rush past her. In sharp, swift movements she began to practice her katas, her chosen form of meditation. In the distance the village children played. Three of them, all the same age of ten, broke away to watch her graceful art. They stared at her metal hands and closed eyes in awe, never having seen anything like it before. Eljun's eyes went wide. "I told you. Nemesis is the strongest. And she doesn't even have her swords!"

Red-haired and freckled Finn shook his head. "It's Titus. He's strong and smart. He's an actual general. Did you see his armor?"

Edda twirled her braids, looking past Nemesis. She giggled. "You're both wrong, it's Tarak! My sister thinks so too."

Eljun tried to copy Nemesis's moves. Edda and Finn chuckled at his clumsy attempt, but he didn't care. "No, it's Nemesis. I don't care what anyone says, it's Nemesis."

"Children!" An adult male voice broke their play, with all three jumping at the same time. The stroppy farmer gave them a stern look and waved for them to come closer. "Back to work. The lot of you!"

The three children scattered towards the fields. Eljun glanced back to see Nemesis walking away towards the rest of the villagers and warriors, returning to work until they stopped for a late lunch. They all knew the stakes were high, and the first part of the day had to be the most productive before the heat set in.

By midday, hunger and heat brought the work to a halt. With many female and a few male eyes glancing in his direction, Tarak removed his shirt to give it a quick douse in the icy river water. He put it back on to cool his skin.

The villagers sat not far away, eating hard cheese, cured meats, and fresh bread beneath a cluster of large trees that provided shade. Despite the approaching threat, they seemed to be in good spirits as they talked amongst themselves. Sam returned to a large basket and pulled out a new sowing project. Aris settled next to her with enough food for both of them.

Hervor approached Tarak with a cloth holding a generous portion of bread and cheese. "Here, you have to keep your energy up."

He looked at the lunch and smiled. "Thank you. I wasn't sure who to ask."

"Don't be shy. You don't get what you don't ask for." She turned to walk back to the group of women who seemed to follow her. He watched her wide, luxurious hips sway beneath the fabric of her trousers. Titus slapped him on the back and leaned close to his ear. "Now that is a woman who could tame a wild beast without even touching it."

Tarak looked back at Titus walking towards the lower end of the river where the banks were covered with high and thick reeds.

Nemesis lay on her back with her hat low, shielding her face. The children who had watched her earlier giggled, talking to each other. Finn gave Eljun a light shove. "Well, go. You like her so much. I *dare* you." Edda nodded in agreement. Eljun held a stalk of wheat in his hand. He crept towards Nemesis on his toes, trying to remain as quiet as possible. As he got closer to Nemesis, he extended the stalk. He looked back at his friends stifling giggles and shooing him forward. She remained still when he turned back to her. Just as the edge neared her chin, Nemesis reached out and grabbed it from his hands with a hard tug. She gave them a stern glare.

Eljun's eyes widened as he shrieked. "I told you she has other powers!!" he screamed, running to catch up with his friends, who laughed as they fled. Nemesis couldn't stop a small smile forming on her lips as she readjusted her hat and returned to her rest.

After lunch they worked until the sun was a bright blister falling behind the mountains. Kora took control of the wagon pulled by uraki. Hagen stood behind her, stacking the dried bundles of wheat Sam, Gunnar, and Nemesis tossed onto the wagon. When the field was clear they all nearly collapsed. Hagen wiped his brow and chuckled. "I might need someone to help me home."

Gunnar and Kora exchanged sly glances. Nemesis spoke up. "I will. Before sleep I'd like to sit in the fresh night air."

"You sure?"

She gave him a short nod without looking at Kora or Gunnar. Hagen walked next to her with one hand on her bent arm. Sam looked around awkwardly. "Well, I better get back to my project. Sleep well." She gave them a smile before turning in the direction of her home.

Kora and Gunnar stood in front of each other with the moons now shining brightly above them. A cool breeze blew her hair in front of his face. "We should probably get a good night's sleep tonight. It's the sensible thing to do."

She took a step closer to him and licked her lips. "I'm not sensible. Fighting the Imperium is far from sensible."

"So where does that leave us?"

She smirked. "Dead and satisfied." She turned in the direction of his home. He followed behind, ready for another sleepless night wrapped in her sweat and scent. The scent that would never leave his skin or bed for as long as she lived. An invisible leash pulled at his soul as he watched her skin glow beneath the night sky. Tonight would be all about making her happy, satisfied, feeling loved.

It was another predawn start in the longhouse. Hagen appeared rested and ready to start a day of vigorous back-breaking work they hoped would save their lives. He banged a tin cup and pan together to get everyone's attention and wake them up. Tarak yawned as he tied his hair back then rubbed his eyes. Hervor handed him a steaming ceramic mug. He smiled and took a sip of the black brew. "What did you put in this?"

"It's a secret. A little something extra for stamina." She gave him a wink.

He took another gulp, looking into her eyes. "Stamina

is not a problem for me. Early mornings are. I prefer to stay up all night. Sleep late."

He handed her the mug back and she took a sip. "Good to know."

Gunnar and Kora were not late, but Den still watched them walk in together from his periphery. Hagen gave the pot one last clang. "I know you all are tired, but we are far from finished. We did an excellent job yesterday. I haven't seen anything like it in all my time, but that says a lot about you and what you can accomplish. See you all out in the fields."

The villagers and warriors made their way out of the longhouse to begin another day of arduous work. Tarak had a better feel for the rhythm of his task. It was mind clearing and soul cleansing. Hervor watched him tie a bundle faster than the previous day and more efficiently. As he began to work on another stalk, a man cursed in front of him. One of the reapers held his broken blade. "Lads, do we have any spare? I don't know how long this will take to fix."

"No. We are using everything we have to get this done on time."

Tarak overhead the conversation and walked towards the reapers, who stopped their work. "May I?" The reaper with the broken blade handed it to Tarak. "Sure. You know how?

Tarak inspected the two broken pieces. "If you have the tools."

"We have a smithy. Hasn't been used as much since Erik has taken on less work because of his age."

"Take me. I'll do what I can."

Tarak worked the metal with the expertise honed from his time in captivity. He hammered it to the right weight and thickness until it was perfect—better than before. There was pride in his eyes as he walked back to the field with it in hand. The reapers cheered while Hervor looked on. Tarak handed it back to the man. The reaper stood and twisted it to get a full view of the blade. "It looks great. Thank you."

"No problem."

Milius stopped their work to look at the new blade. "Do you mind?"

"If you think you can," said the reaper.

Milius held it in their hand. Nostalgia and longing ached in their chest as they closed their eyes. Memory surged like the energy of a comet. The blade belonged in their hands, it was as if they had held it before, long ago. Milius opened their eyes again and took a few steps back. With precise form, they glided the scythe across the tall stalks that fell in a perfect row. They handed the scythe back to the reaper, satisfied they still possessed a part of where they came from. The reapers simply watched Milius, awed by what they had witnessed.

Titus removed his flask from his belt and shook it. There wasn't much left as the contents barely sloshed at the bottom. He paused before drinking the rest until a final drop fell into his mouth. He smacked his lips then looked at the flask, as if he was about to say goodbye to an old friend. He turned his head from left to right to see who might be watching, dipping the flask in a barrel filled with water. He smiled then stomped towards the villagers at rest. "Get back to work. The lot of you!" He took a large swig from the flask knowing he had everyone's full attention. Little did he know Kora stood in the distance and clocked his secret. She felt a swell of pride, hoping he was a step closer to living up to his full potential again, to reverting to the leader he was born to be, the warrior they needed to succeed.

The villagers and warriors continued in the fields, piling the last of the bundles onto the gravity-decks of the wagons until there was enough to start milling in the granary. Kora looked at the building, remembering the night of slaughter that began this journey. Now the farmers tossed grain into the air to separate the wheat from the chaff. She watched it flutter into the air and hit the light. The golden hue of the waning sun made it look like a shower of stars. Nemesis laughed as she smiled with the children playing with her. Small bits of chaff fell into their hair. A slight bitterness washed over Kora, knowing the Imperium still planned to come here. All this work shouldn't be for them. And why still come here? Did someone know she was there? So much didn't make sense, including her feelings for Gunnar.

"We need lifting!" someone shouted. Kora moved into the granary as grain was being poured down a chute and into the gigantic grinding millstone. The stone turned and creaked as it created flour that fell into large burlap bags. A woman tied one of them at the top and looked at Kora. "Just in the back." Kora nodded and lifted the one-hundred-pound bag onto her shoulder to place it in storage.

Gunnar was in there keeping notes on the production. He looked up at her and smiled. "There really is nothing you can't do."

She shook her head and dropped the bag against the wall. She glanced around before leaning in to kiss him, then walked away to grab another bag. But kissing him once wasn't enough. She turned and wrapped her arms around his neck and kissed him again. She giggled like she never had the chance to do on a warship. Even the lovers she took during her many campaigns had taken on a more serious tone. What she felt for Gunnar was like nothing she had experienced before. This was sunshine on her face after a storm.

Soon they were no longer alone as Tarak and Titus were also heaving the large sacks over their shoulders to speed up the process. By the time the sun was nearly gone, the sacks of flour reached the ceiling. Titus and Tarak were covered in specks of flour dust when they dropped the last of the sacks. Tarak gave him a hard slap on the back. "I believe we all deserve a drink. Am I right?"

"Hell yes! Perhaps two," said Titus with a large grin. They looked towards Gunnar, who continued with his notes and numbers. "You coming?"

He glanced up. "I'll meet you in the longhouse. Just finishing up." When they left he stopped his work and looked around the storage room. He wondered if this was the sum of their existence. This was what their lives were worth to the Imperium, or maybe not. He hoped all of this would make a difference. As he left, Aris was returning for another transmission to *The King's Gaze*.

Aris saluted the hologram of Cassius. "How has the harvest been going? Any protests from the villagers? I hope they have been providing you with all you need."

"No, sir. All is to schedule. And nothing to report on the villagers."

"I've not seen Faunus or Marcus during your reports."

"They have been busy driving the villagers, sir. Getting that extra bit of work out of them. They wanted to continue… enjoying the village right now so they sent me."

"Very well. When you see them let them know I would like a word."

Aris swallowed hard but kept his composure. "Yes. I believe it's your phrase, um… every child screaming… every mother crying."

Even as a hologram, Cassius' eyes were as hard and cold as millstones. "That is one of mine, yet I can't take authorship. I believe it originates from our Regent Balisarius himself during his time as a fighting man, and it is my honor to quote him."

"And now mine. The work has continued around the clock and we should have all the grain milled into flour just in time for your arrival."

This good news still didn't move Cassius to a smile. "Excellent, Private. And if the villagers have held up their end, maybe some mercy is in order."

"These dogs deserve nothing but our boot."

Cassius' eyes narrowed. "Is that right? We'll see when the job is done. For the slain king." He put a balled fist to his chest.

Aris nodded and made the same motion. "For the slain king." He saluted Cassius and waited for him to end the transmission.

Cassius turned to the back of the bridge in *The King's Gaze*. Noble emerged from the shadows. "I should have killed that traitorous little shit with his sisters. There is still time."

"If that pleases you, sir."

"It would. It's clear that what the Hawkshaws are reporting is true—that Faunus and Marcus and the rest of his men are dead. The Scargiver and the others are among them. The young private has chosen a side. He shall die with them."

"What should we do, sir?"

Noble paced to the front of the bridge. He touched the scar over his clothing. "We wait for more information from the Hawkshaws. Let them think we know nothing."

"Yes, sir."

Noble knew he had survived for a reason. His renewed determination to crush the rebels made him think back to the time when he truly learned the meaning of what it took to be victorious.

THE JOYFUL SPIRIT OF THE LONGHOUSE HAD RETURNED. MORE VILLAGERS wandered in to meet the warriors. Their conversation filled the space as they shared stories and bonded over the hard work. Sam and Aris arrived together. The center tables were filled with roasted meats and vegetables, freshly baked bread, ale, and wine. The small village band stood at the front of the longhouse playing music made for dancing. Thoughts of the Imperium were worlds away in that moment. The village relished in their united effort to bring in the harvest in record time. They achieved an impossible feat. That should be celebrated, and they did. Before Sam had a chance to sit down, Aris extended his hand towards her. "May I?"

She smiled and placed her basket down. "I love dancing." Together they moved towards the dancing crowd. Milius sat not far away, swigging ale and eating a hearty stew of mutton. They spotted Hagen approaching and raised their goblet. The old man winced as he sat down with his own large goblet of wine in hand.

"You were good out there," he said to Milius. The warrior wiped their mouth with a cloth and nodded. Their eyes softened with thought. "I come from a world much like this."

Hagen searched their face to clarify that what he saw in their eyes would give him hope for Veldt. "What became of it?"

Milius took a large gulp of ale before answering. "The very thing we came to prevent. I look at this village and its people. I can't help but to think of my own home. The ones left behind."

Hagen opened his mouth to speak as a song played by the band ended. He was interrupted by Sam. "Everyone… If I could… I'm sorry, I just…" The room quieted as she spoke and Aris lay her basket on a table next to her. She managed a shy smile and fiddled with her fingers in front of her as she had the attention of everyone. "I… I wanted to well… to welcome our new friends. I wanted to give you these small gifts I've made. I know that you all come from places much richer and more sophisticated than here so I hope they do not insult you with their simplicity. But I've made them with gratitude."

Her eyes trailed to the basket and a beaming Aris. She unpacked her basket with the sewing project that had taken most of her free time outside of the fields. There were stacks of cloth, banners. She took a deep breath for confidence before speaking again.

"When I first saw you all ride into our village, I felt General Titus was like the grand mountains themselves. Strong and unmoving." She took the banner from the top of the stack and handed it to General Titus. The image was a handstitched brown and green mountain that fell into a V-shaped valley. Blue threads recreated the river. He smiled and nodded with pride before bowing his head to her. She walked back to the table.

"Tarak, your spirit is untamable, but your nobility is undeniable, like the snow elk." Sam handed Tarak a banner with a large elk. Its head was held high with sharp antlers and its body took the entire width of the cloth. Tarak also gave her a bow and touched it to his chest. She raised another banner.

"Our own Den is like the land beneath our feet rising to defend us." Den moved through the crowd to meet Sam. The image was of a fertile field with the large Mara overhead.

Den took the banner. "Thank you. And I will defend this land until my last breath."

Sam took the rest of the banners off the table. She raised one with a large sun over a meadow of flowers. "Young Milius shines as the sun upon our faces. Warming us and bringing us comfort. Steadfast and true." Milius stood to receive their banner. They pressed a balled fist to their chest in gratitude and smiled.

Sam moved to Nemesis sitting on a bench. "Nemesis, fierce as the storm with its flashes of lightning but with its life-giving rain. That is the source of life. The storm is the mother of us all." Eljun took the banner from Sam and laid it in Nemesis' metal hands. Tears welled in her eyes with this gift from the heart. A bright yellow bolt in the center looked striking on the black background of clouds. She bowed her head in thanks towards Sam.

Three banners remained in Sam's hand. "Gunnar, you are our heart. You give us hope." The banner was an image of the longhouse. She looked to Kora, who stood next to Gunnar. "And Kora. You are our guardian wolf with bared teeth. You stand between us and annihilation."

Kora took the banner in her hands. Her fingertips touched the image of a wolf's head. Its teeth were bared and eyes yellow. She smiled and paused, gazing into her friend's eyes before embracing her. For the first time, she felt like she belonged to a family again. When Kora pulled away, Sam held up the final banner. "And the strength of us all together. Our fate is bound." It was an image of a bundle of sticks held together by a red string. The cosmic fate that brings individual timelines together.

The crowd erupted into cheers and the band began to play again. Aris placed one hand on Sam's back. "You were amazing. I think you deserve one too. You have this way of touching people. It's healing… like magic."

Her cheeks bloomed with pale pink. "Another dance would be just fine." Aris held out his hand and led her towards the band, where Den had two young women coaxing him to dance whilst they both flirted with him. Eljun had his feet on top of Nemesis' boots as they danced together. His little moon-shaped face glowed with pride.

Tarak spun Hervor around then pulled her back by her waist towards him again. Her fingertips glided over his tanned bare arms. They locked eyes as their bodies moved hip to hip in sync with each other and to the beat of the music.

Kora remained where she stood, observing the villagers and warriors. Feeling the rough cloth in her hand made her want to go back in time and kill Noble all over again. Yet, she felt a sense of bittersweetness at this place she hadn't meant to find whilst on the run. Gunnar had left her side but now walked back with two steins of ale. Her heart ached at the sight of his strong jawline and the thick hair on his face that made her squirm with delight when it brushed against her thighs and neck. He handed her the stein. "You looked like you needed something to drink."

"Did I?" she quipped.

"Yes. And I thought maybe after you finish that we could…"

"Could what?"

"Whatever you want."

She brought the mug to her lips and guzzled the ale without a break. Her eyes locked with his. She licked her lips then wiped her mouth with the back of her hand. The desire in the moment bubbled like ale foam. Their moment was interrupted by the sound of the longhouse horn ringing to the rafters. General Titus stood in the front of the room, holding the horn. He scanned the room as it quieted down then cleared his throat and removed his hat. His voice held the dusty gravel of the Colosseum floor and the dark depths of space. There was longing with every note as he sang a ballad from his home. It was a loving plea to the ancestors, his mother, and the god of his people to send courage and blessings. May the love felt be a protection.

He bowed his head with claps from the crowd. Aris turned to Sam and looked into her eyes when the song finished. He whispered, "Shall we get some fresh air?"

"Okay. We can look at the stars for a little while."

The two walked to the granary and climbed onto the roof with a ladder leaned against the wall. They sat side by side. It was a clear night with the two moons nearly full. "What was your world like?" asked Sam.

Aris looked to the sky with memories flooding back. Most were good, but the only way he had survived this long was by not thinking much about his home. "More moons. It was beautiful." He exhaled a deep breath as he said this with the sorrow and longing inside of him like the song Titus sang.

"Is it not beautiful here?" she asked as she looked him in the eyes and he matched her gaze.

"Yes it is. There are many things I find beautiful here."

Sam averted her eyes and gave him a shy smile with these words. "If we survive… when all of this is over… will you stay?"

He touched her hand and she turned to face him again. "If you will have me. My world is not what it was. Nothing left for me there." With the gravity between them finally becoming too dense to stop or deny, Aris leaned towards

Sam. Their lips met and he kissed her tenderly. "I hope that wasn't too forward," he said.

"It wasn't." Without any hesitation she kissed him back.

Noble stood in front of the large window in his private quarters. He hated being tested, being doubted. Bringing Kora to justice would prove his worth once and for all. It was an undeniable feat of excellence. The one and only time he had failed was the worst and the best thing to happen to his career, because he learned what it truly took to achieve greatness. His thoughts wandered back to those years after the Academy.

Atticus Noble knew his new assignment was a test. After leaving the Academy, to everyone's surprise, he didn't do as spectacularly during his first campaign as thought. He was so sure of his abilities and couldn't wait to make a name for himself without his father being mentioned. It was his time to take over the glory of the family name. Unfortunately, Cassius and he were sent to separate campaigns. Noble was stunned and humiliated. His father even more so. Both parents looked at him with hardened glares when he returned to Moa. However, he was used to that. Both were exceptional in their military achievements. They expected nothing less from him. Noble was a necessary vessel for their DNA, nothing more. He felt the gravity of that his entire life.

His father. Dominic Noble, stood well over six feet tall, his body a chiseled frame that he took pride in. His food intake and exercise were precisely monitored to maintain optimal health and longevity. He had few enhancements because he relished the challenge of pushing himself to the limits as he aged. When he walked into a room, people noticed. His hollowed cheeks and deep sockets for eyes gave him the look of a phantom in uniform that had arrived to deliver a grisly death to the first person he encountered. "Do you know what people are saying about you... *us*? It is an absolute disgrace. And unless you do something it about it... you're on your own."

All Atticus could do was stand there and take in his father's words without protest. His anger and humiliation made him want to reach out and grab the old windbag by the throat until he turned blue. But he couldn't. "What do you suggest I do, Father?"

His father smirked. "There is one place. Maybe you will survive and maybe you won't... We need to make contact with the Vori."

Atticus' eyes went wide. "But they..."

His father stomped towards him. "Don't give me excuses, boy. I heard your excuses as to why you failed. Do you think I got where I am by allowing others to get there first? You need hard lessons. This is your first."

"May I request Cassius to accompany me?"

Dominic's face screwed. "What for? Absolutely not. This is down to you. You have to prove your worth or there won't be any more help from me... ever."

Atticus knew if he didn't come back alive from this assignment, no one would care. You weren't special in the eyes of the Imperium unless you made it so. People killed and lied to climb the ranks. And many more died during their service. His father might even be relieved. If he failed now, both his parents would shun him. He had to live up to the Noble name.

"When do I leave, Father?"

"In two days' time, so don't get comfortable." Dominic left without any further words. It was all down to Atticus now.

The destination was a world known for its organized criminality far from the Motherworld, a place no one wanted to go to. You were lucky to make it out alive. It was under Vori control. The environment on the planet was just as hard as the people who ran it. Winters covered the planet for eight months out of the year. Four of those with blizzard after blizzard. Those who could leave during the harshest months did so.

The Imperium couldn't threaten the Vori, they killed their own without mercy and operated all over the universe. Shutting down their businesses and influence would mean they would have to be hunted down one by one. It was more trouble than it was worth, because the Vori didn't feel the need for heroics or rebellion when it came to the Realm.

The royal family who unified the planet Dobro under one crown had been slaughtered centuries before by the founding fathers of the Vori, who established a tight grip on the people and the planet. All formal religion was banned. The Vori expanded throughout the known universe in pockets of crime from Daggus to Providence. Now Noble had to broker a deal with the Vori to help them retrieve hard-to-find resources that had been already stripped from Moa and other known worlds. The Vori had eyes everywhere and deep pockets. The Hawkshaws were great bounty hunters and the Vori were masters of the black market with a penchant for brutality. Nothing was sacred.

Noble was escorted from his transport by three burly bald men in thick coats. All had misshapen knuckles with fat callouses. One of them had a nose that had to have been broken at least a dozen times. going by the odd shape of the bridge. None of them had the whites of their eyes dyed red. Apparently when the Vori first began, having bloodshot eyes from the initiation proved your worth. People knew you had passed into their ranks with a solid beating by the toughest. Today, only the bosses within the organization could carry this honor. However, the red was a type of permanent tattoo and not from a fight. The thugs next to Noble would probably die before they ever got to that point.

Gregor lounged on a sofa covered with bear skins. His blond hair was slicked back and ended just below his earlobes that both had small gold hoops. He sucked on a hookah, filling the air with eddies of smoke. What should have been the whites of his eyes were red, with a tattoo to match, to mark each stage of his career with the Vori. The black-collared shirt he wore covered most of his tattoos, except for black tendrils that crept up the side of his neck and ended at his jawline. If Noble had to guess, he'd say Gregor was about his father's age.

He looked up at Noble, but didn't rise from his seat. The guards moved to the door. "Sit down. This isn't a place of ceremony or fake pretense."

Noble gave him a nod and sat on an armchair in front of him. "Thank you for accepting this invitation. We have much to discuss about a mutually beneficial partnership."

Gregor grunted before speaking again. "What does a skinny pale kid from a rich family from Moa know about negotiating, or fighting? What do you know of pain and blood day in and day out?"

Noble kept his cool. " I have fought. In fact, I just came from my first campaign. But this isn't about me… the Vori are strong. But not stronger than the Imperium. Do you have a Dreadnought?"

The gangster narrowed his eyes. "No, but we know how to make your life hell. The Vori are everywhere. You can't shoot us all down like you do peasants on other worlds. We would still exist elsewhere. I know how your regent works. We have done nothing to rebel, we only want to conduct our business our way. The Vori do not have *partners*, only associates."

Noble looked at the high vaulted ceilings and gold altar of what was once a cathedral to the planet's original religion. The building was now filled with weapons hanging on racks. "Why are we meeting in a church?" asked Noble.

"Not a church anymore. Those silly ideas died with the priests and the royals who used it to control the people… something *your* people may know about. We put an end to that long before your king. No, this is a place of business. A place where we worship what really matters in this universe. The only authority here is us. Some smoke poison root ash and others believe with all their being in something they can't see. Magic. Both are drugs for the weak minded."

"Well, the Realm is very real. And the slain king deserves respect."

Gregor leaned closer. "You cannot intimidate me and neither can a dead monarch. I have no faith. Only this life, its pleasures and pains. Then there is death. So we do what we want." He stared at Noble and searched his face as he sucked on the hookah and blew smoke in the air. "Now, why are you here?"

Noble remained stoic, wanting to cough from the smoke, but stifled it. He couldn't fail. Wouldn't fail. "I come here with a list of materials we wish to procure. There are resources we no longer have readily available. Some are extremely rare. We recognize your abilities in trade."

Gregor tossed the hookah aside and rose to his feet. He was easily a foot taller than Noble and twice his weight. "Come. There is a fight tonight. Lots of betting. If you feel like wetting your prick, then there is whatever you prefer."

The three bodyguards looked towards Gregor and he gave them a nod. They led the way out of the main vestibule with Gregor and Noble following behind. Once out of the cathedral and into an attached newer annex, they passed a room with a small port window. Noble stopped and his eyes widened as he showed his disgust at the sight. He could hear chirps and slapping coming from inside the room. Gregor stopped next to him. "It takes a certain… appetite to really enjoy the Twins. But when you do you will never forget it. They are at a select few pleasure emporiums, but mostly with private owners."

Noble looked back at Gregor, who chuckled as he walked on towards the transport bay with the bodyguards waiting for them.

They traveled through the city in an armored all-terrain vehicle. The city appeared colorless except for the remining bright spires of the old cathedrals. The Vori didn't bother repainting the ones that had been stripped of color from the harsh weather. New buildings were being erected, but were not aesthetically pleasing. They were functional. Long lines of citizens snaked on the pavements as they waited to receive their rations before returning to their duties. None of them smiled. Noble realized they had already been beaten into submission by the Vori. There was nothing the Imperium could do to them they hadn't experienced before. It was the ones who called the shots he had to charm.

The building they stopped in front of had the appearance of a bunker. The solid concrete rectangle with no windows looked more like a prison than a place of leisure. The bodyguards got out first, then Gregor and Noble followed.

They didn't need to do anything as a mechanical eye scanned them before the double steel doors opened. It smelled of smoke, strong alcohol, and sweat. Fighters of all genders battled in metal cages. No weapons allowed, but no move was forbidden.

Viewers sat at tables while waiters and waitresses in little clothing offered drinks on platters. Some tables had hookahs attached to the side. Most of those seated wore expensive clothing and shoes. Watches and jewels were on show on necks and wrists. Bets were made by tapping on a console on the tables. Those sitting further back could watch the fight on their tables via hologram. Gregor had a booth at the very front. Blood sprayed across the floor. Noble looked at his feet, watching his step. Gregor laughed at him. "Afraid of a little blood? Surely not?"

Atticus straightened his uniform. "No. I am not. I've taught those who think they can best me lessons before. Just wondering how this doesn't get in your drinks."

"Don't worry, boy. We think of everything. And fighting in the real world, not the Academy, is different."

Noble sat down and watched two women pummel each other with their bare fists. Each had a split lip and patches of hair missing. He thought back to the hungry citizens standing in a docile line on the street for rations. He turned to Gregor. "How do you keep order here? What does it really take to break not just an individual, but many?"

Gregor took a glass from a tray and slapped the ass of the waiter wearing tight trousers. "It's simple. Be willing to do whatever it takes to get what you want without mercy. Sacrifice your mother if you have to. If you have a best friend, don't let them know they are as expendable as the next person. And every skin except your own can be handed over. Take what you need from people and places then move forward. Make a name for yourself and let it speak for itself."

Noble nodded. He knew of someone like that: Balisarius. "Thank you for that advice. I shall take it in serious consideration. Now, about our business."

"When do you need to leave?" Gregor asked without looking at him. He watched the fight as the two women screamed on the ground while still exchanging blows.

Noble was taken off guard by this question. "I have been instructed as soon as possible. However, I do not want to leave here without what I have asked for."

"Stay here for eight months with me. You will learn more than that damn school for sheep disguised as soldiers."

Noble glanced at the fight as one of the women screamed in agony. Her arm was broken behind her back with the victor sitting on her thighs, both her eyes almost shut and bloody. A man speaking in a language he couldn't understand stepped into the cage and held up the winner's limp arm in victory. Medics soon rushed in to see to the crying woman with the broken arm. He turned back to Gregor. "And if I do this?"

Gregor clapped with the rest of the crowd then turned to Noble. "Then you will get what you want, perhaps more.

I have questions for you too, though. I do not keep you here out of the kindness of my heart or charity. Nothing is for free. But you will be treated like my guest as long as you respect our authority and ways of doing things. It is not up to you to judge."

Atticus thought of returning to his family and the Imperium, delivering exactly what was expected of him and more. The disastrous campaign would be forgotten and he could take up a place more worthy of him and his family name. His parents would rethink their disappointment in him. He would stay with these outer world gangsters. What was the worst that could happen? He would be a guest.

"I will stay. Thank you for the invitation and hospitality."

Gregor waved over the waiter he liked. When the waiter was tableside, Gregor grabbed the bottle of clear spirits from the tray and an extra glass. "Good, Atticus Noble of the Imperium. We will celebrate tonight. I expect we will get through this all." He lifted the bottle. Atticus watched Gregor fill his glass to the top. "Thank you. I feel we will learn much from each other."

Gregor lifted his glass and gulped the alcohol. Noble did the same, but drank slower and couldn't finish it. He winced and smiled. Gregor shook his head and chuckled. "Oh, what you will become when we are done with you."

Noble shadowed Gregor for three months, through grotty prisons with people sleeping on shit-stained mattresses, swanky clubs where every taboo was indulged, and barren fields unable to yield a decent crop. But as

Gregor liked to say, "hunger makes everything cheap". The dark atmosphere and even darker streets depressed him. At night, packs of wild hound-like creatures roamed the streets feasting on vermin. The decrepit buildings with peeling paint they traveled to for business purposes were the worst he had ever seen for any population. But there was no dissent. The Vori had crushed any shred of hope in their citizens. They were happy with whatever scraps they were given and readily joined the Vori ranks to have a better life.

However, he hadn't received any of the promised information. The messages coming from the Imperium were impatient and curt. His own impatience was building day by day, but he knew he couldn't approach Gregor just yet. The man instilled a fear in him. He hated yet admired that. It was a quality he wanted for himself. Gregor's presence demanded attention. His male and female lovers came and went and sometimes joined him in the room forbidden to Noble. It was where the Twins were kept. The sounds emerging from the closed doors filled Noble with fascination. He dreamed about what pleasures could be experienced.

Noble slept comfortably in Gregor's home. He knew he was being monitored at all times, but never did he feel threatened.

"Get up!" shouted Gregor as he burst through Noble's bedroom door that didn't have a lock. Bleary eyed, Noble looked towards the door. "What is the meaning of this?"

Gregor stood before him, dressed and freshly shaven. The scent of his cologne was only that strong when he had been up all night at the battle bars. "To see what you are really made of."

Noble got out of bed and dressed as Gregor watched. For a moment he wondered if this was the end of him. Did the Imperium do something to threaten the Vori and he was the sacrifice? Even if that was the case, there was nothing he could do. He was trapped.

Two stout bodyguards in thick animal-hide coats stood outside his door. Gregor led the way through the hallway and Noble followed. The bodyguards were not far behind Noble. Something was definitely up. A transport vehicle was waiting, as was the freezing middle-of-the-night air. Again, he had no choice but to follow. They drove in silence for fifteen minutes until the vehicle stopped in front of a building similar to the one they went to when he arrived. Gregor turned to him. "Never walk away from anything. You finish it without mercy. Today you prove you deserve to live another day and are worthy of what the Vori have to offer."

"I am."

Gregor got out of the car with his bodyguards and walked towards the door. Noble knew this would be some sort of test, but what he did not know. The doors automatically opened. It was another club like the one he had been to when he first arrived. Inside were five shirtless men covered in pink scars that made various designs, serving as tattoos. They also had actual black geometric tattoos on various parts of their bodies. They looked at Noble with blood-red eyes. In the center of the ring was a man tied to a chair. He wore a torn Imperium uniform and no boots. The soles of his feet were shredded. His head was covered in a white helmet that only left room to breathe through the mouth.

"This man destroyed my property. He owes me, but he is from a noble family. You must get information from him. I want to know about his father's mining on Daggus."

"Why me?"

"You will find out in a moment."

They walked into the ring. Noble glanced back at Gregor. He cocked his head towards the bound man. "Touch the side of the helmet."

Noble did as directed. The helmet turned translucent. His eyes widened. It was a man a few years older than him, a son from one of the old families of Moa. *Dorn...* He remembered his name.

"Atticus!" The man smiled, showing bloody teeth. He looked relieved to see him. One of his eyes was purple and blue. His bottom lip split. "Please help me. All this is a big misunderstanding. You can tell them. Things are different back home."

Noble had to appear friendly. This much he knew. "Yes, well, this gentleman behind me feels he is owed for damaged property. I will do what I can to set you free."

"She was only the card dealer... I was told she also did other things."

"Okay. Okay." Noble kneeled in front of him. "We will set this right. But first you need to offer this man something in return."

Dorn shook his head in desperation. Sweat and condensation filled the helmet. "Anything."

"Here." Gregor removed a stick from his pocket. "His blood, then his eyes. The edge to prick his finger and the long end to scan his cornea."

Noble rose to his feet and took the metal object that could have been a pen. He walked around to the back of Dorn and jabbed his finger, then moved to face him again. He held the pen horizontally. It scanned his eyes.

"What was that for?" Dorn stammered.

Gregor gave him a half smile as he narrowed his eyes. "I want the company manifest. Now I can get them," Gregor said in a gruff voice.

"What? No. You…"

Gregor's voiced boomed through the room. It seemed to fill every dark corner. "What? I cannot do what when you are there and I am here. I can do anything I want as long as you are there."

Noble handed the instrument back to Gregor, who was smiling. "Now kill him."

"No! No!" screamed the man as he thrashed in the chair.

Gregor leaned towards Noble's ear. "I made it easy for both of you. Just swipe the right side of the helmet."

"Please! I beg you! We are almost family on Moa!"

Noble stepped closer to Dorn. Without hesitation he swiped the helmet. It remained translucent but the mouth hole shut. The man's mouth opened and closed as wide as his one good eye as he gasped for air and screamed.

Gregor and Noble watched him die as the many shades of suffocation colored his face. Noble felt nothing, except to think, *Better Dorn than my own skin.* Gregor tapped him on the shoulder. Noble glanced back. Gregor held out the instrument again. "Now you."

"What? What for?"

"I said on your arrival I wanted something in return. I want what secrets your family hold. Your parents are very high ranking. That is useful to me for avoiding Imperium eyes when needed."

Noble knew this was the test. How deep did his loyalty lie, and to whom? If he didn't do this, his parents would consider him a failure if he was sent back with nothing. If he did, he would betray them, yet go back victorious. Either way it didn't change how much they loathed him. He owed them nothing. He had to do this for himself because one day they would be dead. For a moment he imagined what his father's face would look like in that helmet. Noble grabbed the instrument and did to himself exactly as he did to the dead aristocrat slumped in the chair.

"You will be marked now. It only stings a little."

The sound of soft buzzing moved from behind him to in front of his face. One of the shirtless men held a small box. Noble tried not to show fear. He failed. The box was ring-sized. The man opened it. Inside, a small four-legged insect-like bot jumped to life. The man brought it closer to Noble's cheek. It jumped from the box onto his face and scurried just below his eye. Noble grit his teeth as it made tiny bites. It felt as if was burrowing into bone. He couldn't see what was happening, only feel it. Pain seared across his eyeball, causing it to throb.

His hands curled into tight white-knuckled fists. After a few minutes, it jumped back into the box. The man held the box to Noble's face. In the reflection of the metal, Noble could see a small geometric black tattoo had been left behind.

"We celebrate!" shouted Gregor. The man was always ready to put a substance into his body.

"And then we start work? You have what you want now and what you promised me?" asked Noble.

Gregor searched his face and narrowed his eyes. "Yes, amongst other things."

Noble paused. "May I make a request?"

Gregor arched one eyebrow and pulled out a hempil leaf cigar. "That's bold. You can ask."

"I want to meet the Twins." Noble looked Gregor dead in the eyes as he said this.

Gregor folded his arms and laughed. "I knew when you arrived you had the disposition for what they... offer. You know, if you were not one of them you could have been one of us."

Noble glanced at the dead aristocrat being pulled from the chair by Gregor's men. His body would probably be taken to one of the factories outside of town, never to be seen again. "Is that how it is? Such a clear division?"

Gregor grinned. His red eyes seemed to glow brighter as if aflame. "Always... You must think like that. Operate like that, and you will go far."

Noble walked out of the building determined to be as hard as the Vori, to obtain Gregor's secret to being a dominant leader of men. By the end of the night he hoped to open the forbidden door that led to the slithering bodies of the Twins.

THE MORNING SUNLIGHT BURST THROUGH THE VALLEY TO WAKE THE VILLAGERS. Despite the celebration the night before, their work was not finished. The bell rang out in the distance.

Tarak stretched his long limbs before cradling the woman next to him. Hervor smiled, feeling him close as he kissed her bare shoulder from behind. "We should get up," she said with a moan.

"Really? With this?" He pressed his body closer to her and moved his hand to her hip.

She bit her lip with his erection teasing her from behind. For hours the night before he had made her body feel like she hadn't in years. And what she lacked in youth, she had in experience. For so long it felt wasted, until now.

Her inhibitions and insecurities had fled as the years rolled by. Very little made her blush in the bedroom. "How can I refuse the pleasure of *that* again? I think we have a little more time… the first bell is only a wakeup call." She turned towards him and pushed him onto his back.

With a lustful gaze, she looked at his chiseled body and smiled, knowing what some of the villagers whispered about him, his striking looks. Her tongue and mouth traced the ridges of his smooth chest and belly, that rose and fell in anticipation as her loose hair trailed after. His eyes snapped open and his mouth opened to release a long groan as she took him all the way into her mouth. He looked down to watch her use her tongue and lips with abandon, with quick flicks and deep gulps, while her fingers created a titillating magic of her own between his legs.

She didn't leave an inch untouched. When satisfied with his arousal she crawled towards him to sit directly on top of him. "Where did you learn to do that?" he quipped.

She smiled and chuckled as she began to move her hips. "I was married for thirty years. You learn to keep things exciting and you learn about yourself… what you like."

He gripped her hips to guide her grinding as she swayed at just the right tempo to make herself moan. His hips bucked to be in sync with her. She moved his hand to touch the remaining soft flesh exposed between her legs. It made her cry out further until the tension couldn't be contained any longer. She trembled in ecstasy.

Tarak tightly clasped her hands and continued to thrust, watching her pale skin turn pink from the glow of orgasm and her breasts softly bounce. His body spasmed and released with the explosiveness of making this moment count. It could be the last time either of them felt this again. They both collapsed with only minutes to spare before the bell would ring. Another reminder of impending doom.

After the second gong of the bell, the villagers began to gather in front of the longhouse, where Hagen stood next to Titus. "Alright. Today we begin the preparation for our defense. We start by moving the grain into the village, so they can't shoot us from orbit without risking its destruction. Then the weapons left behind by the Imperium will help us hold our ground. Gather and account for every hunting rifle, every knife, every round of ammunition in the village, along with every Veldtian known to partake in the hunt. Take all your weapons to the granary. The river... That is where we will take our stand. Those who aren't working will practice shooting or combat. We will assign the weapons to those who prove the most adept. Finally, Kora and Aris will retrieve her dropship. Questions?"

The villagers looked at each other in silence with no one having much to say.

"Let's get started then." He watched them rush to find weapons. Hervor still had her late husband's rifle. Others scoured sheds, barns, locked chests that had not been opened for years.

Milius helped the villagers haul sacks of flour from the granary to various important points in the village, including in front of the longhouse. They formed a long row of sacks, piled high. From above there would be no clear way to avoid destroying all the much-needed grain. The village children watched on in curiosity and a little fear. The revelry of the completion of the harvest had fled. The final phase, the one that might lead to their demise, had begun.

Hagen left the bell to join Titus, Kora, Gunnar, and Aris in the granary. Gunnar was accounting for all the weapons in the the same way that he kept account of the grain. Most of the large crates left behind by the Imperium remained unopened.

"I wish Jimmy was here. He would know all about this stuff. I was just beginning," said Aris.

Kora inspected the crates. "I'm sure he is okay and perhaps closer than we think." She noticed a bar with a sharpened point at the end. "Only one way to find out. Let's open these and see what we are working with."

She pried open one with Titus and Gunnar helping to pull away the loosened wood with their hands. "That's the last of it," she said, looking at the weapons.

Titus nodded his head in approval. He picked up a large rocket launcher. "This will do nicely." As more weapons were uncovered, his eyes went large upon seeing a blunderbuss. He put the launcher down for the other weapon. "Now we're talking."

Gunnar went to work laying them out and keeping tally. Not long after, villagers began to arrive with weapons in hand. Hagen graciously accepted them and laid them with the others to be accounted for. "And the uniforms of the men left behind?"

Gunnar pointed to a pile of folded clothes on a barrel. He walked over them and held one up. "Blood won't come out easy, but we can try."

Kora glanced at the fabric. "No. Leave it."

"Right. I will get the targets ready. We have the weapons, now we need to know who will use them," said Titus.

Gunnar looked up from his paper and pencil. "There are quite a few scarecrows in the old uraki barn, plus bales of hay to pin targets. I'm sure you can also find used bottles at the longhouse."

Titus took one of the weapons with him. "Good. Those will work just fine."

Kora looked to Aris. "Let's go to the dropship."

The warriors set up targets in various stations in the fields with Hagen on a gravity-deck handing out weapons to those who knew how to use them. Scarecrows propped on spikes with old clothing blew in the breeze. Cloths with crude targets drawn on were pinned to stacked bales of hay and old glass jugs stood at attention on more bales of hay. Sam scanned the weapons before picking up the blunderbuss. She walked into the field with an empty target, an ugly scarecrow in a tattered shirt and trousers. Her eyes searched the target before aiming and pulling the trigger. The chest burst open with a flurry of hay and insects before falling to the ground.

"Impressive." She turned to see Titus bowing his head. He walked on to see more villagers using some of the Imperium weapons and the old rifles found in the village. Their ability was better than he expected for farmers. Hay and glass filled the atmosphere with the pop of ammunition. Tarak stood near Nemesis with a group of villagers being taught the basics of hand-to-hand combat with a blade. Even little Eljun, who had become Nemesis' shadow, watched on. Milius had a scythe in their hand as they demonstrated various moves to use in a fight. The metal sliced the air in large arcs. The villagers copied their movements with enough distance to not catch each other. There were also pitchforks propped on bales of hay to be used next. Titus made his way to Tarak after seeing the progress the villagers had made.

"Are you ready?" Tarak asked.

Titus took a deep breath and a swig from his flask. "One is never ready for battle. Battle takes on a life of its own. We will see."

When the villagers moved on to practice on their own, Eljun looked at the blades and chose one. He showed it to Nemesis, who watched him. She inspected the blade. "This is a good one."

She couldn't help noticing him not looking at the knife. "What is it?" He averted his eyes. "Why do you always wear those gloves? Is there something wrong with your hands?"

Her eyes softened. "These are my hands. If I took them off, I could not hold my swords or anything. That is the price I paid for waking the knowledge in my blood, which showed me the way of oracle steel. Together they create a source of tremendous power and reasonability."

"Should I get gloves too? Will they make me stronger?" He looked into her eyes with the innocence only a child possesses.

"You don't need them. You have your own strength and in time you will find your own path." She handed the blade back to him with a smile.

"Thank you." He cocked his head and continued to look at her.

"What is it, child?"

"Do you have children somewhere?"

Nemesis gave him a little smile, knowing this question was not meant to inflict pain even though it did. It reminded her of her own children's curiosity when they were alive.

"I did. But they are no longer with me. Perhaps one day I will see their faces again and join them wherever they are."

"Oh. I hope so too… I guess you will fight for them… to see them again."

"I fight for you now so that you may live a long and good life."

Eljun moved closer and wrapped his arms around her waist and embraced her. "Thank you. I know you won't let us down."

. . .

Kora and Aris left the granary for the dropship. It wasn't a long journey, which was good because they had no time to spare with the fight nearly on their doorstep. When Kora could just see the ship through the trees, she rushed forward. She stopped just before opening it. Memories washed over her. Her heart broke all over again, remembering the events that led to her bloody departure. She swallowed hard before burying her emotions. Now wasn't the time to dwell. "How'd you fix it?" she asked.

"It wasn't me. Remember that Jimmy we brought? It was him. I think he also set us up with food one night at camp when he fixed it. He's like this silent guardian in the forest. I wish he would join us. No one would harm him."

"Let him come to us. Come on, let's get this back to the village."

Kora opened the ship whilst steeling her nerves. She didn't think she would ever be inside an Imperium ship again, let alone part of a rebellion against them. Her fingertips hovered over the controls.

"I can do this if you want," said Aris.

Kora looked ahead and gripped the controls. "No. I have to do this."

The ship roared to life and lifted from the ground. Part of her lightened, as if she had come full circle. This could be the beginning of the end or a new beginning. She set a course for the village and raced off. The speed and adrenaline returned to her body as she remembered how to maneuver. Aris watched her with intense concentration, soaking up everything he observed. When they hovered above the end of the field near the bridge, she landed the ship. She exhaled as the ship came to a stop and she swiped the motherboard to open the ramp. Titus and Tarak stood on the bridge and approached Kora.

"One final weapon… You in that ship," said Tarak.

She smirked. "Pray it works."

The Hawkshaw stood at the cliff's edge observing the village with high-powered binoculars. He had targeted the dropship. Two other Hawkshaws organized their supplies and weapons for their continued surveillance until the Dreadnought arrived. They all wore thick pelts as the climate had an uncomfortable chill for their species. "They have a dropship. Prepare to transmit. This is something *The King's Gaze* will find interesting."

"I hope interesting enough to pay more."

The Hawkshaw in charge looked at his first in command. "Just get the transmission ready. We will negotiate at another time."

The Hawkshaw nodded and turned on the hologram. The transmission blinked red as it went through. Then Cassius appeared within the glass. He seemed agitated, which was a first. "What is so urgent that it couldn't wait until your normal report?"

The leader glanced towards the two others, who sniffed the air. He turned back to Cassius.

"Sir, the village has an asset. We just discovered they have a…"

The transmission ended.

A deafeningly loud blast burst upon them, and shards flew in the air. The Hawkshaws looked towards the shots fired. They were all stunned when Jimmy appeared with sharpened horns on his head and his cloak floating in the wind. Two large strides and he had the leader's neck in his hands. He smashed the Hawkshaw's face against a boulder, then the transmitter.

As he fell to the ground, a Hawkshaw unloaded two rounds towards Jimmy. They bounced off of his metallic body. Jimmy rushed towards him and backhanded him hard, knocking the weapon from his hands. Jimmy turned to the other Hawkshaws and fired. Both fell to the ground, dead. Jimmy surveyed the equipment then looked towards the village. This was very bad. The Imperium had to know everything the village was planning. The Hawkshaws were excellent at what they did and lived up to their reputation.

Anura. Home world of the Anuran species, who were especially adept to Hawkshaw work because of the evolution of their unique features and abilities on their world. The lowlands of Anura were green and wet with high humidity. Vast jungle and wetlands made the world nearly impenetrable in some parts. Large carnivorous plants the size of an average human bloomed from the muddy banks, while tangles of vines were home to fierce animals and poisonous insects. From the sky, part of the planet looked like a green cocoon. The Anura knew how to navigate the harsh environment, using it to their advantage in battle and for everyday needs.

They were just as tough as their world. Their mottled skin could be used as camouflage: some from the deepest jungles could change their skin color when in fight or flight, or could trigger bioluminescence. Their upturned nostrils could pick up scents that others could not detect and their yellowed eyes worked well in the dark. It was essential. Anura was either thick jungle canopy, murky water, or darkened caves.

The Anura lived in clans with an alpha female and male who assumed leadership based on their ability to battle for the title. It wasn't just single combat. They had a small army that battled with them. Whoever had the least casualties and survived took control of the clan and their lands. They had their disagreements, but the clan elders did agree on one thing. Outsiders were immediately slaughtered. This edict came to pass as an alien species attempted to make contact, but instead spread a fungus that decimated thousands of Anurans and indigenous wildlife. It took decades for them to repopulate.

Their mating was unique to their world and species. There was no intercourse between the male and female. The act enjoyed by humans repulsed them, thinking humans filthy. The female emitted strong pheromones some would call unpleasant when her body ovulated. The chosen male would sit in a rock pool in underground cave water. He closed his eyes and fell into a meditative slumber. This allowed his body to give his seed the energy they needed to excrete from his body and survive. The living tadpole-like creatures swam in the cool waters until awakened by a female. He would leave the water, so up to ten females could sit inside the same pool with their legs spread. They would fall into the same meditative slumber for hours until none of the male seed remained.

When contact was made after that, any alien force was slaughtered and their technology taken. This created their own tech from whatever they salvaged to serve their way of life.

And then there were those in the mountains. The terrain moved from low elevation to rolling highlands that were cooler. This is where the dead were taken to return to the earth, as well as any invaders and unwanted tech to be burned or buried. The land knew best how to cleanse. No one lived there because it was sacred ground. It was also devoid of any cover from above, leaving them vulnerable. Only wildlife and stone temples had to endure the storms that brewed at the highest peaks of the highlands. Then it sloped higher, the land turned rocky and barren with snow, ice, and frigid waters that in spring flowed to the lowlands.

The Anura who dwelled at high altitudes had lived there for so long their skin had become thicker, mimicking the color of rock and snow. They were also larger, to accommodate for bigger lungs in the highest of altitudes that would kill a human in hours. Any outsiders who wandered their way died from the harsh elements of the mountains or in the jaws of the Sherpanura (as they were called). They developed their own culture and rituals that centered around the mountains.

When the Imperium first landed on Anura hundreds of years before, they killed thousands in the lowlands, believing them unevolved animals. Acres upon acres of jungle blazed. However, the clans united and killed Imperium soldiers with stealth. Beasts beneath the surface of the swamps pulled many soldiers to their death without a trace.

The stings of arm-length insects tossed out of their hives by the destruction caused chaos amongst the soldiers. The bullets hit some, but the insects were not easy targets as they darted through the air. You can't kill what you can't see coming.

The only source of sustenance the Imperium soldiers could rely on were the supplies they brought. It was hard to tell what could and couldn't be consumed by humans, after what looked and smelled like sweet fruit caused a handful of soldiers to vomit until they could not stand.

The Anura could digest the fruit, however. Through their vomit, the humans served to spread the tiny spores that created more of the plant. The mechs that stomped through the jungle in pursuit of the Anura were crippled by what seemed like invisible forces. Their heaviness made them sink into the wet earth and they could not be retrieved. The Anura led them to the places they knew were not stable enough for the weight of the mammoth-sized machines.

Admiral Juno had two minds about this species as he surveyed the damage they caused. They could be obliterated out of the universe from space, but this would mean returning from a campaign empty handed with a lot of collateral damage. Senate seats and career advancement were made by successful campaigns. And Admiral Juno needed a win. He watched his men disappear into the jungle and not return, and it occurred to him this species could be used in another capacity.

This species were natural hunters who acted on their feet, and they looked terrifying. Admiral Juno had his remaining troops retreat to a burnt clearing. He knew they were being watched. The soldiers remained at the back of the clearing with their weapons close, but not drawn. He had crates of supplies unloaded in the center of the ashen clearing. The sun blazed and loud croaking from the giant amphibians indigenous to the world filled the air. He looked around, feeling every drop of sweat bubble from his pores. The Imperium uniform was not made for such an environment.

He lifted his hands with palms facing forward and began to speak, knowing they would not understand exactly what he said, but hoping it might bring one of the leaders out. "I know you have eyes everywhere. This is your land. I want to speak. And I offer a gift."

With Admiral Juno was a young scribe from the seminarian whose job it was to gather information about non-human species. He was taught to extract it by any means necessary. On Anura, he already had done his own dissections and probing, causing the greatest body count to date. He did his best to translate based on the language of Anura they had captured and killed. There was no response from the depths of the trees. "The crates," he said to the darkness. A soldier moved to open the crates and removed bottles of the admiral's finest alcohol from Moa and other delicacies. The second crate was filled with weapons. "Gifts! Let us be allies and not enemies. I have underestimated you." Admiral Juno gave a short nod to his enemy, watching and waiting.

There was a rustle in the distance. Out came two of the Anura, who appeared like the other warriors they had encountered. There were blades strapped to their bulky legs and arms. One had a type of rifle made from different tech slung across his chest. Both wore loincloths made from amphibian skin. They walked across the mud until they faced the admiral and sniffed the air. One of them grabbed the cured leg of meat with the hoof still attached at the end, and the other a bottle. "May I?" Admiral Juno took one of the bottles and opened it. He took a large gulp. Both Anura sniffed towards the bottle. They turned and walked back in the direction they came from.

Admiral Juno smiled. "Make a fire," he told the soldier. "I think we have a bit of a wait before we settle this."

When the dense stars looked like flowing silk in the night sky and the temperature dropped to almost pleasant for humans, a torch of fire blazed in the distance. The admiral looked up and stood to greet, who came his way. There were ten of them. In the back was an Anura who had to be the leader. He held the bottle and walked slower than the others. The admiral tapped the scribe to wake. The group came to a halt when they were face to face. The leader stepped forward.

"I speak some of your language. Traders, trappers landed here when I was very young. My father's father kept one to teach me their technology and language. Then we killed him and made him an offering for the Sherpanura."

Admiral Juno smiled. He glanced at the bottle. "Did you enjoy that?"

"Not particularly. We have our own. But my warriors do… What do you want here? You have done much damage to our world and killed many innocents. It is a disgrace how you fight."

Admiral Juno could not believe the boldness. "So have you. Many of my soldiers died terrible deaths. That is why I want an alliance. The Imperium could use warriors like yours. Not for the battlefield to wear our uniforms. Other work, suited to your abilities. I like the way you hunt. You can offer something we do not possess."

"We are good at what we do. It is our way of life. But fighting for sport is not."

"You mentioned the Sherpanura. What is that?"

The leader glanced back. "Those who live in the mountains. Like us, but not interested in anything but their world up there. Their ancestors explored and never came back. Every few seasons they come down at the highest and brightest moon to choose females who are willing to go. We keep the peace. Do not go up there. They would

destroy the entire mountain range under your feet if you

attempted contact, even if it meant none of them would be left alive."

Juno could barely see the peaks of the mountain range in the darkness. "I see. When we arrived it did appear like there were large stones up there, not part of the mountain. I took it as nothing."

"That is your problem. You thought nothing of it. Those are temples. That is all I will say about that."

Admiral Juno didn't want to press his luck. The others were inconsequential if they kept to themselves and were hostile. He had incurred enough losses already. "Thank you for being so honest with me."

"Now your turn. What do you want. Tell me in plain words."

The admiral looked at the male and female warriors next to the leader. "I want a few of your warriors to come with me for training. If they do, we will leave you in peace on the grounds we will occasionally return for any others who wish to join our ranks. They will see places well beyond your planet, as beautiful as it is. They will have more of any of these things we offer." He stepped away from the supplies.

The warriors looked on in curiosity. The leader walked towards a weapon in a crate and picked it up. He inspected it before tossing it down again. "We cannot do this until it is light. We will call everyone out. Then we will see who wants to go. Wait until I arrive."

The leader turned and walked back into the jungle. The mist rising from a nearby lake blew across the dirt, shrouding their exit. Admiral Juno exhaled, feeling proud of this turn of events. He could hear it now, his name being whispered in the halls of the Senate. Their leader said fighting was not their way, but he didn't believe that. The ones he took with him would incite fear just by their look. They would also be trained to be loyal, and to want more of what the universe offered.

1

NIGHT CREPT OVER THE VILLAGE WITH THE DARKNESS OF A VELVET CAPE. CLOUDS covered the moons and stars, leaving no light. The longhouse stood alone as it gave the village some illumination. The exhausted villagers retired for the evening, leaving the well-fed warriors sat around a single roaring fire in the longhouse. They stared at the crackling flames jumping as the fire consumed the logs. The wood glowed from the inside until it split and crumbled. Fire spared nothing within its reach.

"I've never been one for giving speeches; however, we are on the threshold of what will test us down to the white of our bones," said Titus. He glanced at each of the warriors one by one. "We know what each of us must do. You're here because I want you to know who the hell you're fighting with. Everyone must share the truth… I'll go first and I will begin on Sarawu. It was a beautiful place. I dreamt of removing my uniform, fading away into the lush forest and joining the local people there. But that was not to be."

Three low suns hung like vigilant bloodshot eyes in the sky above Sarawu. Their tears bled into the horizon as they set and gave the atmosphere an ominous glow. General Titus stood in front of the hologram on his Dreadnought waiting for Balisarius to speak. He had just been told the people of Sarawu held a vote to declare independence from the realm. That knowledge made it perfectly clear why he had been sent to make their presence known, but not engage. But the people of Sarawu showed their bravery and thirst for freedom by voting for independence. Knowing the outcome of the vote made him nervous.

The wage of war is peace because peace cannot be bought with war. All that is left are dead bodies. They can neither create nor contribute in any way. And that is what they had learned in all their weary days and nights of screams and mortar shells. Different world, same goddamn shit. Titus felt boiling defiance. Fuck the piety of the Motherworld and their arrogance, the lust that knew no bounds.

General Titus' Dreadnought was shot from the sky with a salvo of cannon fire from warships of his own fleet. When the blitz was over, the Imperium sent an entire regiment to hunt him down. Titus and his troops fought until their guns were dry. It wasn't enough.

When loyal troops cornered a battle-weary and blood-spattered Titus on the ground, he lifted his hands in the air in surrender.

The barren land had been stripped by fire, the hulking wreckage of a Dreadnought Titus once commanded smoked on the horizon. Nothing lived, only decay and ash. Birds were replaced by dropships screaming across the plains, continuing to pockmark the ground firepower. General Titus crushed bone and branches beneath his boots as he marched with Motherworld rifles aimed at his back. Was he the only one left? He set eyes on a Dreadnought above his head. His heart might as well have been riddled by a firing squad.

On the ground an even greater horror. What was left of his regiment were on their knees, hands bound behind their backs and black rough sacks with the image of a giant eye and single tear over their heads. He could see their heavy breathing from the way the fabric sucked in and out of their mouths. He could sense, *feel* their terror. He hated that he wasn't next to them. With the sound of thunder, the Dreadnought unleashed its lethal justice upon the soldiers as Titus watched.

"No…" he whispered until it was a scream. Their bodies became ground meat as they exploded. Blood saturated the parched soil. His grief was a Dreadnought rising from the pit of his stomach to his fists. He shouted a war cry of despair and hate. What had he really devoted his career to? With everything he had left, he ripped his wrists apart with a hard yank, snapping the cuffs that bound him.

He spun around and knocked the soldiers closest to him to the ground. Before the others had time to react, he had one of the soldiers' weapons in his hands. His shouts rivaled the sound of the rapid fire cutting down the Imperium soldiers who caught him. He didn't stop until he ran out of ammunition. His chest heaved as he cried for his men, his tears merging with the sweat riding down his face. Titus didn't want to glance back at the dead. That moment was seared into his memory for the rest of his days. He scooped up extra weapons, all he could carry, and began to run. He was now and forever a wanted man.

When Titus finished his story, the only sound was the all-consuming flame in the fire pit. His eyes glowed with its light. "Never again. I'll never surrender. You should understand that today, before you choose to follow me tomorrow." The rest of the warriors nodded after he said this. The room remained silent until Milius stood.

"Thank you, Titus, for your honesty. I admire that. I have never fought in a battle like the one that's coming. I was raised in a place much like this. My home world was called Meadai. My childhood made me understand that the land is not the growing of food, but the cultivation of the tribe itself.

"When the ships appeared in the sky above my world, I looked to my tribal elders for how we would respond… They cowered before the might of the Realm. Submitting and giving them everything because they were too scared to fight. They said, 'What can we do against the might

106

of the Motherworld?' There was little room left to be a child when the ships arrived. And I too saw those I cared for die."

The morning mist always settled over the mountainous terrain with a freshness and soft dew. The moisture and warmth during the day made it fertile ground. The farmers began early on the steep fields on the mountainside. Large scythes cut through stalks with a rhythm perfected over generations. Through the patchy cloud cover, a Dreadnought made its way above their village. Seventeen-year-old Milius worked with the rest but stopped to watch the hangar release several dropships. Before anyone could react, the large circle of carved stone ancestors that rose to the sky were obliterated from above. Rock burst through the air and fell across the field and those working there.

The villagers looked at each other in terror before abandoning the fields for the village center where the dropships landed. Milius followed the crowd, hoping to reunite with their father. Dropships whizzed through the air as if they were trying to herd everyone in one place. And they were: the village square. By the time the chaos subsided and the villagers were mostly in one place, an admiral stood with the their mayr and six other tribal elders. He turned to the fearful villagers with nervousness.

"The council has met with officers from the Motherworld. This is Admiral Wurst. For now, everyone return to your work. At first light we will meet here again. Anyone disobeying these orders will suffer severe consequences," the mayr said.

Admiral Wurst had the look and heft of a hungry gray mountain bear. He eyed the village children and women with a lust that made Milius sick. Henna, their best friend, leaned close to their ear. "How are we supposed to work like everything is fine with these invaders? What do you think they will do?"

Milius shook their head. "Do as we are told. The council will know what to do. Maybe they will come to an agreement then leave."

Henna looked at the others their age, who returned to work on the steep mountainside as instructed. She stepped closer to Milius and spoke quietly in their ear. "I want to hear what is going on. Let's listen by the back of the tribal hall."

Henna walked quickly with Milius following. They could see Admiral Wurst heading back to his ship and the tribal elders walking as a group to the hall. The rest of the villagers tried to appear as if they were resuming their normal duties; however, it was obvious they were hovering near the hall and elders to catch any bits of information.

Henna and Milius went through a storage room attached to the tribal hall. The door between the two wasn't thick, and voices could clearly be heard. Milius opened it a crack to see. The tribal elders looked like children as they huddled around a table.

"This isn't good. Look what they did to the stone circle. We can't allow them to take what they want. It will never be enough," said a council woman.

The tribal leader shook his head. "Exactly. Look what they have done unprovoked. We absolutely have to cooperate. What good will come from fighting, but dead bodies and even more destruction to our fields? We will starve or have to leave, at least those that survive. We have nothing that can come close to taking down those ships. They have weapons that can kill us by the dozens. We don't fight."

"So we sacrifice our children? You are okay to pay that price... their blood?"

The six other elders murmured as they spoke amongst themselves. The leader couldn't look the council woman in the eyes. "If that is what it takes. Do the rest of you agree?"

The council woman stared at them hard as they averted their eyes. "Aye," they said one by one.

"I will tell the admiral himself. I will tell the village tomorrow about the new work schedule. Every eldest child will be sent off world."

The council woman spat on the floor. "Cowards. You will all die anyway. We all will."

Milius couldn't believe what they were hearing. They glanced at Henna. Tears streamed from her eyes with a look of hate across her face. "We have to fight." Before Milius could stop her, she ran from the storage room. Milius followed her, dashing around the hall and to the front to catch up with the mayr. "You can't do this! We must fight. I will not be sold like a goat for your freedom! Do you even know where they will take us?"

The mayr stopped. "Go home and spend the rest of the time you have here with your family. Causing trouble will only make it worse for everyone."

"No!" she screamed. The council woman approached the two. "If they don't fight, maybe others will."

Milius stood in shock hearing this conversation, not knowing what to do. Soldiers walked around the village with weapons in hand, observing everything. He could see the admiral step out of his dropship and look in their direction. "Henna, we should go," said Milius.

She shook her head. "I'm going with her."

Milius opened their mouth to speak when their name was called. "Milius." They looked back to see their mother. Her eyes appeared like she had been crying. "Please come home. I don't want you wandering around with all these soldiers." Milius looked back to Henna. "Milius," their mother called again.

Henna stepped closer to Milius. "Go. I will keep you posted." Milius smiled at Henna despite feeling torn. They trusted Henna would come to the house in the morning. "Alright, see you soon."

The following morning a light drizzle fell and thick fog covered the mountains. It added to the somber confusion of the village as they waited for news. The mayr stood in front of the villagers again, appearing ten years older. He looked like he hadn't slept a wink all night. His voice matched the weariness in his eyes. "The council has decided to be in partnership with the Realm. In exchange for our labor, produce, and homage the Realm has generously offered their protection for all good tenants on their land…" He paused with his lips pursed as if he could stop the following words from escaping his mouth. "And every family must part with their eldest child. The Realm requires strong backs for work on another planet."

There were gasps and cries. Milius shook as they glanced towards their father. Admiral Wurst stepped forward. "I knew you would react like this. So let me show you what happens to *partners* who do not cooperate…" He turned and nodded his head towards a soldier, who left the waiting regiment. From out of the dropship he brought one of the elders, badly beaten. More gasps. The dropship lifted to reveal four large cloven beasts being held with neck reins by another soldier. They whined and kicked at the noise of the crowd. Usually they were used in the quarry for moving stones due to their strong legs and back. They could also be ridden, but were not very fast.

The elder was marched to the center of the horses. Soldiers tied ropes to his ankles and wrists. Tears fell from his eyes as he averted his gaze, but remained silent. The mayr refused to look in the direction of the unfolding horror. Admiral Wurst walked over to the horses and patted its long mane while the soldier poked the elder with the butt of his gun to encourage him to lie down. With arms and legs outstretched, Admiral Wurst raised his hands and slapped the beasts so they ran.

In an instant the elder had his limbs torn from his body. Blood and exposed bone was all that could be seen besides his dead eyes staring at the sky. The drizzle turned to rain, causing his blood to run from his torso towards the feet of the observing villagers. Admiral Wurst turned back to them. "By midday I expect the eldest from every family to be here. The Imperium has steady work for you to add to the greatness of the Realm and continued expansion."

Milius embraced their father. "I will see you again. I promise."

"Don't make promises you can't keep. Come, let us have one final meal together."

Henna approached Milius and their father. "How can you eat at a time like this? We have to do something if the council won't. They are sacrificing us to save their own skin. We should be fighting."

Milius' father glanced at the admiral and the mayr, who were looking in their direction. "Keep your voice down, Henna. You will only make things worse."

"I don't care! I'm getting others. Maybe we *need* to fight for ourselves."

As Henna began to walk away, Milius took a step, but their father grabbed their arm. "Let her go. Nothing will come of it."

Milius stopped and watched the admiral follow Henna with his eyes. Their father squeezed their arm. "Please… we don't have much time." Milius looked back. His aging eyes pleaded. They couldn't leave that way.

The following day, screams and shouts erupted from the square. Milius had been preparing to leave, hoping Henna would show up. She never did and a strict curfew had been placed upon the village. Their father rushed into kitchen. "You have to get on that Imperium ship."

"Why?" asked Milius.

"Just do it!" he shouted. Milius could still hear the commotion. They ran past their father and out the door towards the fray. Milius stopped. Henna was on her knees, beaten and bruised with other villagers. Some lay on the ground with bullet holes in their heads. Milius screamed without thinking of the consequences. "Are you the eldest child in your family?" A soldier dug the butt of their rifle into Milius' back.

"Yes!" shouted Milius' father. The soldier pushed Milius towards a ship with the bay doors open and a line of villagers waiting to board. Tears streamed from their eyes. They didn't have the heart to look back at their best friend, dear brave Henna, or their father. He meant well, but this couldn't be how it ended. The sounds of the village became warped and didn't make sense. Nothing did. It was like a nightmare come to life.

Milius boarded a dropship in a numb haze, to be taken to a foreign place to create more wealth for the Realm. Those who were too weak, ill, or old to work were killed without mercy in the village and their bodies dragged to a ditch to be buried in mass graves. The reality of Milius' new life in a labor camp was far worse than being quartered by a horse. By the age of twenty, Milius had spent their last few years in a mine. The gas mask left deep cuts and painful rashes from hours of wearing it in the heat. Anyone who couldn't keep up with production was exterminated, just like before they left Meadai.

Milius had become nothing but a body for the Imperium. When they died, no one would care. They thought of Henna, her courage for standing up for what she believed and dying for it. Perhaps that end was better than collapsing on a foreign world from coughing up blood or sheer exhaustion. Three years of their life was stolen in the labor camp until it all changed with the blast of dynamite that sparked their purpose, their sole purpose.

The explosion threw Milius off their feet along with the others working next to them. Shouts and shots could be heard but remained unseen behind the dust from the exploded rock. Milius scrambled to hide behind the metal cart on hover tracks. Their heavy breathing fogged the mask. Milius ran towards the entrance of the mine to see better, and ripped off the mask. Dying didn't matter in that moment because they considered themselves dead already in that life. As the dust settled, they could see men and women not in uniform savage the Imperium soldiers. The mystery assailants left the workers alone. They had pain across their eyes that added to their ferocity.

Hope and pain surged in Milius' heart. The vengeance they harbored now manifested in this dark Imperium tomb in the form of these unexpected fighters. Not a single Imperium soldier was spared. The one who had to be the leader stood in the center. He placed two fingers across his heart and looked Milius in the eye before glancing at the stunned miners. "You are free. We will do what we can to help you escape. Tell others about this day… about rebellion." Milius caught his eye again. The fighter walked over and extended his hand. "What's your name? Where are you from?"

Milius took his hand and rose to their feet. "Milius. From a world called Meadai."

"I'm Darrian Bloodaxe from Shasu. I have heard of your world. I wouldn't suggest you go back."

Milius nodded, feeling sick about the fate of their father and those left behind. But their misery and Henna's death couldn't be in vain. They still had strength in their bones and a developing bitterness on their tongue. "Then let me fight with you. I have nothing to lose anymore."

Bloodaxe held their gaze. A beautiful woman who looked similar to the tall, muscular man in battle gear approached. "Brother, we have lost a few, but this battle was a victory. I'll be waiting near the dropships to help the captives take over this place and escape. See you when you are finished here."

Milius wiped their face with the back of their hand. "Sounds like you are down a few."

"We are. You know how to use any weapons?"

"No, but I'm a fast learner. Take me with you, please."

"Alright. And you don't work for me. We are one, family. No individual is better than the other."

Milius threw the gas mask to the ground as they followed Bloodaxe from the mine and towards the Bloodaxe ships.

Once on board, they were given clothes meant for training. But Milius didn't want to just take off the gross Imperium-issued work clothing. They wanted a fresh start. Milius took a straight-edged razor to their scalp and chopped their hair off to the skin, leaving only a centimeter. They felt free and ready for whatever the universe had in store for their future, now that they felt they had a future. One that would at least end at some point with meaning, for Meadai and Henna.

When Milius finished their tale, they sat down again. "My camp was liberated by the resistance. And I found a new family who showed me another way. When the time comes, I'll give my life to protect this village if need be because mine never had the chance. I will stand and offer my life for these people… because the people of Veldt have shown a bravery I wish my people had shown.

"I wish my people had the strength to know when to take a stand. To know when to ask for aid. Not to lay down their lives. To stand and die for a place to call home… what more honorable end could one hope for? Henna and a handful tried, but it wasn't enough. More had to believe and work together. My father would be Hagen's age."

Tarak placed a hand on Milius' shoulder and nodded.

The group looked for the next one to share their story. Nemesis broke the short silence. "I had a life before… long before, it seems. Now, I choose the way of the sword. It was a beautiful day. The sun was warm and my children were with their father… we were a little fishing village."

Her metallic hands gravitated to the two metal swords hooked to her waist. She closed her eyes, feeling their energy, remembering the day they came into her life and the course of her life changed forever.

Byeol sat by the sea and the wealth of the ocean provided what the villagers needed for themselves and to trade. Most of the year was pleasant with the sea breeze perfect for drying fish and seaweed. It was a place of peace, but it wasn't always. Nemesis' ancestors from the distant past were people of war. It had never crossed her mind to take a life, though. There was no need.

Nemesis sent her husband Min and their children out on the boat to collect reed eels so she could sell the wooden figurines she carved herself. It required her to travel to the neighboring village. It was nearly sunset when she began to make her way back to her own village. The sound of rumbling could be faintly heard in the distance, but she didn't know what it could possibly be as the clouds had rolled in and darkness was descending. She had to get back to her family faster.

The horror began as she entered the outskirts, glowing from fire. The aroma of burned flesh and wood was a pungent, stomach-churning combination. The roads were impassable in their destruction and filled with debris. She jumped off her cart and ran until the smoke sent her into a coughing fit that made her choke. When she stopped to look around, the village was decimated. The bodies lay strewn across the ground like when the algae blooms killed fish. The houses were razed. It didn't appear like a raid because boats and belongings remained. It was slaughter for the sake of it, or some sort of retribution, for what she did not know.

War was supposed to be a thing of the past, a way of life from which they had healed. Yet now it had been brought upon their heads unprovoked. This village had become a grave. Then panic struck. Her family. She ran towards the estuary. Perhaps Min and her children were hidden and would remain safe as the soldiers moved away from the water.

The best place for them to hide would be in one of the many boathouses; however, she could see fire blazing from that direction. Soldiers must have set them on fire to prevent any means of escape. She continued deeper into the outlying woods to avoid being seen, until she stumbled upon a forgotten shrine and the mouth of a small waterfall. The stone demon shrine held two large blades in the air with its long tongue falling to its belly. The eyes were empty dark sockets. Moss and ivy grew over the altar its clawed feet stood upon. It was from the days that had been long forgotten, until now. She touched its hideous face, the swords.

She had to hope Min could keep their children safe, but there were no weapons on their boat except for what was used to gut fish. Even if there were, Min was not a soldier. They didn't belong in this war. Their village was for fisherman, not whalers with large harpoons and hooks.

Nemesis kneeled and prayed behind the wet shrine as smoke rose to the sky in the distance.

Nemesis crept from her hiding spot hearing neither explosions nor voices. The skies were still lit with fires burning brightly. She hurried her pace towards the estuary where they kept their boat, the best spot for catching eels.

Her heart pounded as she waded into the water. She pushed at the reeds in her way. Just ahead she could see an overturned boat. She rushed towards it and turned it over. Nothing. She continued to wade in the waist-deep water. Three mounds bobbed in the water. Her legs and arms pushed hard against the water with her clothing dragging her back. She didn't have to overturn the body to know it was her daughter. The body had a necklace around its neck. She deluded herself anyway, for a moment. Perhaps she had mistaken the necklace under the Dreadnought-dark sky.

Nemesis grabbed the arm and pulled the body close to her. It was her daughter, without a doubt. Her entire body quaked with sobs she held in as tightly as she embraced her daughter's dead body. The agony of grief ripped her apart in that moment. Nothing else mattered as she held her daughter's small body. There was a single bullet through her daughter's head. She held onto her as she grabbed hold of the other bodies. They were her sons. They were her miracle children she didn't think she could have and those heartless monsters took them from her.

She looked around the dark waters for Min, but saw no sign of him. She dragged all three children out of the water to the bank. The earth was soft around there. She couldn't carry them all back to their home so this would be their final resting place. As she searched for an appropriate place to dig, she found a discarded shovel. This and her bare hands would have to do to create proper graves for them. They deserved nothing less. Beneath a tree, she began to dig until her arms ached. She clawed at the sandy soil with gritted teeth and groans. Stray rocks scraped her hands, causing them to bleed. She wanted the Imperium to bleed too, more and more the deeper and harder she scraped at the soil. Every single person or creature who aligned with the Imperium she wanted to inflict pain upon.

Her eyes stung from her silent incendiary tears. When the hole was large enough, she climbed out and stood above her children. This was the final goodbye. She kneeled and removed the necklace from her daughter's neck. The shape of the pendant attached to thin dried river reeds resembled oracle steel carved in marbled jade and obsidian. She placed it around her own neck as she sobbed. One by one, she ripped strips of cloth from their clothing before placing their bodies in the grave with care.

They came into this world not long after each other and they would remain together forever. Perhaps in another dimension they continued to laugh like a spring rain and fight like little snapping turtles. She kissed their cheeks then climbed out to fill the grave. With whatever sticks she could find, she created three markers and attached the cloth taken from their clothing. She took one last look at the dark soil and walked away.

She shuffled to her village, numb. If soldiers found her then so what? What could there possibly be left to live for? The village was ruined. The homes were razed to the ground and bodies were littered everywhere, with fires still burning bright. Her people did not exist any longer. When she came upon her own home it had not been spared either. But something survived besides her. It was her birthright, a powerful ancestral gift, a rectangular wood box with images of ocean waves and demons rising from their crests.

She opened the box and inhaled deeply. Heat rose from the pit of her pelvis and continued until it hit her cheeks. A sense of knowing and urgency cleared her mind of grief. Inside lay two large identical blades of oracle steel and two metal gloves. They vibrated with memory of the past despite being cold. She knew what she had to do. The way of the demon demanded it. She had never spilled blood, but now she would spill her own because the bloodlust of her ancestors lived in those gauntlets. She lifted one of the blades out of the box and closed her eyes. She inhaled and exhaled whilst trying to focus on the wind and distant sound of water. Chimes that clung to life on a rafter rang with the lightness of the ghosts of the past come to guide her.

She raised the blade, opened her eyes, and chopped her left hand clean off just below the elbow. She gritted her teeth, fighting back a scream as blood sprayed in thin streams. With a trembling right hand she lay down the blade and took the left metal hand out of the box. The metal came alive with four red screws that molded to her wound. A wound that would remain forever more.

She flexed the digits as it ceased to be separate from her skin. Her blood awakened the gauntlets and the steel. This was her new skin. Her metal left hand grabbed the blade from the box and didn't hesitate as she severed her right arm. To her surprise it didn't hurt as much. A numbness, a coating of metal, shielded her pain for the moment. She placed the blade down and attached the other metal glove to the stump that was her right arm. The glove molded itself to her flesh as it did with the other arm. She splayed her metal fingers, reflecting the moonlight.

She peered down at her severed hands. They seemed small and distant. Weak things not capable of what she now wanted to do with these new hands and swords. She picked up the blades. Metal magnetized to metal. Nemesis stood and looked towards the still-smoldering estuary. There had to be places that remained untouched where she could gather supplies for life on the road. But exhaustion made her muscles feel heavy and mind fog made her thoughts confusing. She would go back to the shrine and sleep there. She wandered through the village thinking no one was around, but she was wrong.

"You there!"

She looked up to see a soldier approaching her. She ignored him and kept walking. He raised his weapon and pulled the trigger. In one swift movement she lifted her right sword and deflected the bullet. She looked at the steel in wonder. It was as if it guided her arm, not the other way around. Her new metallic hand tingled with energy. The rage she felt traveled from her fingertips to her shoulders. The soldier fired again. Nemesis deflected his bullet again and rushed towards him for the attack without an inkling of how to fight. The ancestor's blood and steel guided her.

Ancient muscle memory sliced at the soldier's right arm. He screamed as it fell to the ground with his weapon still in hand. Nemesis lifted both swords and beheaded him, both blades slicing across his neck. She watched the blood ooze out of his body as the head rolled to the side. Not a twinge of remorse moved inside of her. He could have been the one to kill her children and missing husband. This scum deserved nothing less than to wet her blades. She lifted the swords that glowed red.

Nemesis finished her tale with her metallic hands on the pommels of her swords.

"Like an abandoned shrine with the elements of nature taking root and growing freely all over, my pain became my rage… my rage became revenge. These swords became my path out of grief and with each arc of these blades, the numbness grows a little bit more bearable and the horror of that day feels further away, where it was the constant tormentor on my shoulder whispering dark words.

"But since that day I've been a creature of revenge. To cleave their hearts in two my only purpose. At nightfall tomorrow I will have my chance. More of their swill standing before me than ever before. All mine to send to oblivion. And yes, yes I will kill them. But it will not be for revenge. It will be for these people. The people of Veldt, who for the first time since that day have given me a yearning to live."

The fire crackled as it died down. Tarak stood, threw in another log and stoked the fire. "None of us get to choose our parents, and mine happened to be a king and queen. My father, the king, had insisted on presenting our terms to the armies of the Motherworld himself, and in answer, they returned his body with the promise of invasion. My mother told me then, a boy doesn't become a man until his father dies and a prince becomes a king. It was the last time I cried.

"Soon after, their ships darkened the sky. For honor's sake, she did not run. I wanted to stay, protect her, but the queen knew to preserve the bloodline and the throne. I was smuggled off planet. Hidden in a refugee transport bound for a near bright star."

The ritual of the funeral procession had been practiced for centuries. Every king had been buried in the same manner as the previous one. Hundreds of nobles and common subjects paid their respects because he was a loved king. A choir sang a hymn that exalted and placed a blessing over the royal family. Tarak watched his father's body, dressed in his royal suit and covered in white bennu feathers, as it was carried on the shoulders of the First Regiment of the Royal Spears. They wore leather belts with a large bennu embossed on the waist.

His mother cried next to him, dressed in all black with black lace covering her eyes. She mumbled a prayer. Only Tarak could hear the bitterness in her voice. The rage she could not show, but at least her eyes were covered so as not to betray her thoughts. Tarak wore ceremonial black bennu feathers across his black suit. The time had come for him to no longer be a prince and become king. They stopped when the body reached the altar at the front of the nave. She reached out with a limp hand and touched the body. With the weight of a sword, the grief sunk into Tarak's body. He placed his hand next to his mother's.

"My son," she croaked. "A boy does not become a man until his father dies and a prince… a prince becomes king." She bowed her head and Tarak's fist balled as he gripped the shroud. His father should have still been alive. He was murdered. Murdered by Imperium degenerates. His father left Samandrai in a hurry. The Imperium gave them no time to respond or negotiate demands. He huffed and argued with the council trying to persuade him to not go to the Motherworld to plead their case and present their terms. "I was not raised to cower before power-hungry regimes who know nothing about our world or people. We deserve more respect than that. We do not serve the Motherworld over the needs of our own people."

"And you are the one to tell him so?" Tarak's mother countered in private with her voice raised and eyes wild.

He paused, lifted one of her hands to his lips and kissed it. "I am king and the one who must be in immediate danger. I must be the one to do this. It is what I was born and raised to do."

Tarak remained silent because there was no use in trying to convince him otherwise. That was the last time he saw his father alive. His ship returned with an automatic destination guidance. He lay on the floor with ligature marks around his neck and his eyes bulging. A single tooth had been removed from his mouth.

They preserved his body so his family and council could see his face exactly how he died. In his hand he held a scroll. The Imperium would invade. She turned to Tarak, who looked at his dead father in horror. In his ear she whispered, "You are the continuation of our bloodline. You are the throne now."

He looked into her eyes. "What are you saying?"

She swallowed hard. "You know *exactly* what I am saying. I will arrange everything and you must go now. After the official funeral, stop wearing all royal clothing. When the time comes. Be ready."

He nodded and left his mother. His thoughts were a jumble. A puzzle of duty, honor, obedience, fear, the agonizing idea of running. But he was the only heir. There was just enough time to bury the king before preparing for war. But Tarak prepared for something else. The following morning after the funeral, he donned the plain clothing of their people.

The entire city was in chaos as it was bombarded from

the sky and invaded on the ground, Dreadnoughts making their way into their airspace and dropships beginning their descents. It meant only one thing: total annihilation. Tarak rushed to his parents' royal chamber to say goodbye to his mother. She stood on the balcony that overlooked the city, the place she loved and ruled with her beloved husband. She still wore her funeral attire.

"Mother."

She looked back at him and smiled with tears in her eyes. A morbid peace radiated from her. Tarak took three steps towards her as she climbed on top of the balcony and hurled herself to the ground. Even if he had stopped her in that moment, she would have found a way to end her life.

She wouldn't be taken alive only to be humiliated or used by the Imperium. She knew the stories of how they operated. The home she knew would be destroyed whether she lived or died. His gaze followed the Dreadnought as screams from the terror below filled his ears and drowned out everything but his hate. He turned to leave for a refuge transport that would smuggle him to safety. Nothing remained for him there.

Tarak paused and looked at the fire when he finished his tale. "I lost my mother and my world that day. I ran for duty's sake for the preservation of a kingdom and bloodline that no longer exists. I was robbed of the chance to defend my people. But no more. When we

REEEL MOON

finish here, that is where I will go. Home, to atone for misplaced honor."

Tarak sat back down. The circle remained silent until Titus leaned forward and looked directly at Kora. "Kora, we haven't heard from you. What's your story?"

She could tell by the tone in his voice and the look on his face he wasn't satisfied with their previous conversations.

"I am a war orphan. The discipline of a military life suited me. I served on a ship much like *The King's Gaze*. Never having a family, I believed I had found one. That is until I arrived here on Veldt. This place taught me what a home and family could really be."

She stared into the fire, but could feel Gunnar looking at her. He didn't betray her trust.

"Hmmm," said Titus, who had a slight smile on his face. "Anything else you'd like to add?"

Kora paused before looking him in the eyes. "No."

Gunnar cleared his throat and raised his hand. Titus motioned for him to stand.

"Thank you all for coming to my village and giving us hope." He scanned the group, looking at them individually with sincerity in his eyes. "I don't know what will come of us all by end of day tomorrow. I can only pray that your pasts will burden you less."

Gunnar glanced in Kora's direction then looked away. She remained stoic.

"Well, I'll drink to that!" said Titus as he raised his flask and took a long gulp.

"How is the spring water?" Kora snapped.

Titus pretended not to hear her, but Tarak did a double take. "What?"

Kora didn't make eye contact with either man. "For several days now, Titus pretends to drink because he doesn't want us to know how much he cares about the coming battle."

Tarak walked towards Titus and grabbed his flask from his hands and took a swig. He brought the flask in front of his face. "It is water!"

Titus opened his hand to take back the flask. He glanced towards Kora and smiled. "Old stories can be hard to give up when you live with them long enough… like ghosts."

"Or demons," Nemesis chimed in.

Kora nodded and met his gaze. "Yes they can."

Hagen entered the longhouse with the tension of the impending battle visible on his face. "The village is ready."

General Titus stood. "Good. Whatever handful of troops they send down to collect the grain, we take them. With all our strength in the field, with no mercy, sparing none who set foot on your land."

"And then what? Negotiate a trade? You think they would listen?" asked Hagen.

"I do," said Titus before looking towards Kora. "But if all should go wrong, as it well may… You've seen to it that the dropship is still in working order and hidden from view?"

"I will." Kora said.

All the warriors rose to their feet to prepare themselves for the incoming Imperium soldiers. Tarak approached

Titus. The two men had bonded and could speak to each other as friends. Tarak screwed his face, surprised more than anything. "Water? Really, Titus?"

Titus tapped the flask on Tarak's chest. "That's General Titus to you…" He looked at the flask one final time and placed it on one of the longhouse tables. This battle was like no other he had to prepare for. At long last, he would face the Imperium. Perhaps, in some way, they would answer for murdering his troops just for standing up for what was true and right. Tarak grinned as he watched his friend leave.

Kora rose at sunrise to get the dropship out of sight. She knew the perfect spot. The caves behind the waterfall were only known to those who had traveled to them. It was far away enough not to be seen, but close enough to get back to village quickly. She scanned the landscape that filled her with an ache. This had to work. She prayed for a miracle. The dropship had to slow on its approach towards the cliff face. Snow from the mountains provided the valley with fresh drinking water and fertile fields, as well as creating this magnificent waterfall that was pure power as it shot down the cliff edge.

Kora guided the dropship through the water and into the mouth of the cave. Mist swirled around the engines as it landed. Kora emerged from the ship and stopped to admire the golden sunlight filtering through the water and cool mist. As she turned to leave, a shadow caught her peripheral vision. She swung around with her hand going to her hip where her gun rested. Behind the water was a silhouette of a man, or a creature. It had giant horns and what appeared to be a cape. It also held a staff. Kora took a step forward when the stranger moved around the falls. Kora couldn't believe her eyes. It was Jimmy. He had changed. Her body relaxed and her hand moved away from her weapon.

"Hello, James."

Jimmy stepped forward. "You know, the last person who called me that was the old commander of the Mechanicas Militarium as he died in my arms."

"I'm sorry. I know we are supposed to be used to death. But it's never easy."

"It's okay. I like the way it sounds. It makes me feel something other than hopelessness. You see, I was given memories of a world I will never see. Loyalty to a king I cannot serve and love for a child I could not save. But the sound of my name as you say it lets me feel even in the smallest why I exist at all."

"Is that why you saved Sam?"

"I am not certain. I know only the thought of her being hurt or destroyed opened a part of me that had been closed."

Kora stepped closer to him and gazed at the changes he made to himself, the wildness of it. "You're choosing a side, James. You and I are alike, designed to kill for them. Understand their nightmare is you and I fighting, not because we are ordered or commanded, but to defend something we love."

Jimmy's eyes seemed to glow brighter as he spoke to Kora. He glanced towards the dropship then back at her. "Let me show you something."

Jimmy led Kora outside the cave. They walked a few yards until she had to lift the back of her hand to her nose. She knew that stench. Jimmy kicked large branches with leaves covering the bodies of the Hawkshaws. Next to the bodies was a smashed transmitter. She scanned the camp and the pieces of broken tech. "How long?"

"Yesterday. This is the transmitter they were using. I'm certain they were in communication with *The King's Gaze*. By now they know everything."

Kora nodded. They both looked at the dead bodies of the three Hawkshaws, already bloating, covered with leafy branches. "You know you can't win," said Jimmy.

Kora turned her attention back to him. "Probably right, but I die at least on the side of honor."

Jimmy's eyes glowed slightly brighter. "Is there still such a thing?"

Kora searched Jimmy's face. The only part that could be perceived as human were the small holes for eyes. Other than that, she saw an impenetrable blank shield. But there was more there. His actions showed that. His transformation was further proof.

"What do you feel, James?" she asked as she focused on his glowing eyes.

"So many things. It is all new."

She held his gaze for a moment more then pointed at the transmitter. "Can I take this with me?"

"Absolutely. I don't know how it will help, but please do."

Kora took a discarded sack from the Hawkshaw camp and placed the transmitter inside.

"I better get started back down to the village. It's a bit of a trek. Do you want to come with me?"

"Thank you for the offer. For now I can probably do best in the shadows."

"Understood. I hope to see you again, James." Kora extended her hand towards Jimmy. He reached out and shook her hand.

Kora left knowing she had to make good time back to the village. The air felt crisp and the sun warm. Alone, she could gather her thoughts. Perhaps that was why Jimmy wanted to remain in the forest. When Kora made it back to the village, she walked straight for the longhouse, thirsty and wanting to speak to all the warriors. She passed Tarak speaking with Hervor on the bridge. "Get the others and meet in the longhouse."

He nodded and rushed off. Kora continued on, not knowing what to say. She would wait to see what Titus' assessment would be.

She laid out the pieces of the transmitter on a table. The warriors stared at it. "How much do you think they know?" asked Tarak.

Kora shook her head. "We have to assume they know everything."

All their eyes gravitated towards Titus, who had his arms crossed, with one of his index fingers tapping on his bicep as he stared at the transmitter. "Then it won't be enough to fight defensively. We have to bring the fight to them."

Milius had a wary look on their face. "What do you have in mind?"

"I'm thinking back to a battle when I first began my career... trenches. We need to regain an element of surprise."

"And explosions. There should be some left behind in those crates," added Kora.

Titus turned to Tarak and Milius. "I need you two to run to the fields and start digging like your life depends on it... because it does." He turned to Gunnar. "We need some sort of cover for the top."

"Yeah, I can grab a few of the villagers to see what we have."

Titus nodded. "Go now." He turned to Kora. "I trust you with the weapons."

"On it," said Kora.

The flurry of activity brought the villagers out of their homes to observe what was happening. Those strong enough helped create a maze of trenches across the field. Tarak heaved soil with the speed of a machine as sweat poured from his body with the sun beating upon his back. Villagers worked behind him to reinforce the wall with wood as he dug his final trench. Gunnar stood not far away, pointing towards him with two villagers carrying materials to cover the trenches with before disguising them with dirt. Tarak glanced over at Titus to see his reaction to their trap. He didn't appear overly convinced, but there was no time or manpower to do anything else. This had to work.

He walked over to the trench and moved the top to give the villager an explosive left by the Imperium soldiers. "Careful now."

Titus turned to inspect the other trenches. The man held the explosive in his hand with a look of concern before placing it in a small hole within the wall of the trench. It could be detonated by hand. Titus returned to see how it all looked. He kneeled and extended his hand to the man to help him out. As he lifted the man out of the trench the sky darkened. Both turned their faces upwards. A Dreadnought broke through the clouds. Titus scanned the village as the bell began to ring in a quick succession of loud gongs. "Take your positions!" shouted Titus.

Kora and Nemesis were carrying lumber towards the longhouse when the Dreadnought came into sight. "The time has come," said Kora as she glanced towards Nemesis.

Nemesis looked to the sky, "This isn't right. I should be down there with the rest of you."

"You are the best of us. They need to see your strength."

Nemesis looked to the sky then towards a group of children and elderly villagers making their way into the longhouse. She nodded as Kora handed her the rest of the lumber in her arms. "I have one last thing to do."

Nemesis laid the lumber in front of the longhouse door as she spied little Eljun sneaking away from his friends in the direction of Kora. She could see in his hand a blade that reflected the sunlight. She stepped in front of Eljun before he could run off. "Where do you think you're going?"

The little boy was startled by her voice and promptly placed both hands behind his back. He looked up at her with naïve innocence, but still held himself with confidence. "To fight. To defend family."

Nemesis already knew the answer, but she still asked. "With what?"

He bit his lip then showed her the blade. It was a small hunting knife with a handle made from snow elk horn. She took it from his hand and inspected it, especially the blade. She tapped the tip with her metal fingertip. "Impressive. Who sharpened this for you?"

He gave her a wide grin. "I did."

"And you did a fine job. I have no doubt you would fight with honor. But we need you here."

He nodded as she handed the knife back to him. "Keep that safe."

Eljun ran back to the rest of the children. Villagers and warriors began to scramble to do their duty. Those who could not fight hid in the longhouse. Sam and Aris helped the adults pile furniture against closed doors and windows. They glanced at each other with nervous energy as they entered the unknown together, not knowing if they would survive that day.

Kora walked into Gunnar's house with more determination than in any other battle she had fought. Now it really counted. Her death would mean something—perhaps there would be some sort of redemption in it. She grabbed an old pair of shears in his kitchen then walked into his washroom. She stared at her reflection in a mirror on the wall in front of a basin on a wooden cabinet. For so long she hadn't felt proud of how she left the Imperium. She wanted to look into the mirror and feel hope again. She lifted the shears to her chin-length hair and made the first cut. Her hair would be in the style of the Imperium soldiers, close to the scalp and not a distraction to the task at hand—to kill. Her black locks fell away, as did her fear to die for what she believed what was right.

INSIDE THE CONNING TOWER OF THE DREADNOUGHT, CASSIUS AND NOBLE gathered their officers before their descent. They hovered over a holographic map in the center of the mapping table. Cassius' eyes focused on every detail. He pointed at a small mound. "That's interesting. These formations are new."

Noble leaned in closer then smiled. "The grain. Look. They've moved it to the center of the village and piled it against the buildings so we can't destroy them from the air." He pointed to different locations. "And there and there. Stacked them as cover to shoot from."

"Clever," said Cassius.

"Hmm. And certainly not the plan of a farmer. Seems General Titus has not drunk all of his wits away just yet."

One of the officers stepped forward. "If I may..."

Noble and Cassius nodded. He pointed to bright red spots on the map. "Look here. Thermal imaging shows clusters of people in the longhouse at the top of the village… no doubt their women and children."

Noble stared at the bright red cluster with sinister blood lust. "We'll do what we can to forestall a pitched battle in the village. While we negotiate we'll dispatch the Krypteian to capture the women and children. Then we will see how motivated they are to fight."

Cassius nodded. "I will begin preparations." He turned to the officer on the right. "Dispatch the mechs."

Five dropships and two flying carriers prepared to land in the village. Two large mechs, beetle-like machines built for battle, rose from the bowels of the Dreadnought on a platform to be attached to the flying carriers. The hangar doors opened. The dropships and the flying carriers flew at speed out of the Dreadnought towards Veldt. When they entered the atmosphere, the dropship carrying the Krypteian Guards landed in the forest just outside the village.

The lead Guard, Cadmus, watched the seven other Krypteia march out of the dropship and stand in formation. He had a mean look, they all did. "I'm under orders to focus on women, children, and the infirm. We want to make sure they are afraid of us enough to stop any rebellion. Don't slaughter them until I give you the go ahead. The admiral needs them alive… just for a little while." The guards looked straight ahead, hearing their orders. "Let's march!"

The four other dropships and two flying carriers zoomed towards the fields just outside the village. The sound of their approach filled the atmosphere and whipped the wind. Only the four dropships landed side by side in the freshly harvested fields facing the river. Birds scattered and small animals raced away. The village remained still. The heavy ramps hissed as they opened and extended across the ground. Within seconds, booted footfalls of seventy-five Imperium soldiers hit the metal with loud thuds. From the first dropship, Noble strode out followed by three masked priests, a scribe, and Noble's six personal bodyguards.

He made his way towards the stone bridge with Gunnar and Kora walking towards him. Her cloak blew in the breeze and across her now-bare neck. Her feet wanted to freeze when she saw the face she thought she had left on the rocks. The entire village remained silent and unmoving at this critical moment. Admiral Noble had a smirk on his face when his eyes met Kora's. Kora calmed her shock and continued to walk towards him with determination, every step taking her closer to her fate that was sealed the day she fled.

Gunnar walked behind, allowing her to take the lead. She stopped five feet in front of Noble, still holding his gaze. His lips curled into an arrogant half smile, but his eyes scanned the village behind her. There were no signs of the villagers. Even the uraki were absent. "What's this? No welcome party? No warm embrace? You know, I've still never shared that cup of ale," he said while he continued to inspect the village. He stopped when he saw a now clean-shaven Gunnar. "But look who is here. The ambitious farmer getting his chance to stand for something."

Gunnar remained silent. Noble turned his attention back to Kora. "Arthelais. What honestly are you expecting to achieve here?"

She clenched her jaw. "The same thing as the last time we met. I kill you."

"Yes, and what an honor it was." Noble lifted his hands to the top of his tunic and began to unbutton it. Kora looked on with curiosity, not knowing what he was doing undressing. When all the buttons were undone, he opened the tunic revealing a thick, puckered scar where she had plunged the femur into his chest. Her eyes focused on the misshapen flesh.

"A scar… from the Scargiver herself."

She raised her eyes to him. "It's ugly… Disgusting, really. Just like you. When I kill you again, there will be no coming back."

Noble scoffed as he buttoned his tunic and shook his head. "Of all places, this is where you choose to make a stand? In doing so ensuring its destruction and yours." He raised his hand and gave his signal. In unison, the soldiers raised their weapons aimed towards Kora. She remained steadfast and defiant as she took a step closer to Noble.

"I have no fear of the Motherworld and certainly not of you. Tell me. The name… Atticus Noble. You wouldn't happen to be the son of Commander Dominic Noble?"

Noble was taken aback by this question, the mention of his father. This was his mission and his glory. Not the man he had always been compared to. He had to measure his answer. "What of it? What of him?"

Her face softened with sarcasm and she threw back at him the smugness he liked to give others. "I am coming to understand now how someone as incompetent as yourself was placed in command of a Dreadnought. That is all."

His eyes narrowed as he seethed hatred. He had few weak spots except for the one she had just pressed. "We shall see who is incompetent when the smoke clears and your village has been reduced to ash in the shadow of *The King's Gaze*."

"Or perhaps when *The King's Gaze* lies in smoldering ruin. I will offer you one chance to avoid slaughter. No blood need be spilled here today."

"You naïve thing. You do realize what the regent Balisarius will give me when I bring you to your knees before him."

"I know men like you. A seat in the Senate is what you seek, I would imagine. If so, take the grain you need to feed your men on your voyage back to the Motherworld. No more and no less. You leave the villagers unharmed and report to Balisarius that the warriors you sought evaded capture."

"And we take nothing?"

"You take your lives. Balisarius will be displeased, but he will not kill a Dreadnought admiral. At worst you'll be reassigned to some remote outpost from where you can begin to work your way up the ladder. Sooner or later you will still have your seat in the Senate. Not tomorrow, perhaps not ten seasons from now, but that day will come. Your bloodline ensures it. This is your choice. Disgrace and relegation, or your head cleaved from your shoulders, your ship serving as your tomb. Your families and all of the Motherworld to know that you were slaughtered by peasants of the Veldt."

Noble didn't react to her words. His icy stare remained fixed on her until he shifted his eyes to her muddy shoes, her cloak, the steel in her eyes and her shorn hair. For a moment Kora wondered if her words had penetrated his ego.

"You think you've given me a choice." His face contorted to reveal his monstrous nature and loathing. "You haven't. I have been tasked with bringing honor to the Motherworld and I intend to see to that task to the end. What amuses me most is that you think you have any power to negotiate. You think I don't know that you're hiding your women and children? Even as you stand here talking to me, your plan is already failing."

Kora remained stoic as she held her ground. Noble took a step closer. Now he would push her weak spot until she caved or bled. "Unless, perhaps, a different bargain could be struck. We take what you offered, the grain for our journey. We do as you ask, leaving the villagers with their lives… The cost of these concessions would be you."

Kora still didn't flinch, but Noble grinned, seeing she was thinking about what he had just said. "Yes, it is true that every member of your rebellious band would be greatly treasured by the Imperium. Yet there is no denying that the one most sought by our honorable regent is Arthelais herself. Therein lies *your* choice. Surrender yourself to me and your friends will be permitted to live. If you refuse, those this village holds most dear, the children and elderly at present sheltered in the longhouse, will be slaughtered by the men on their way to them now. Has enough blood not been spilled in that beautiful building? Are you truly prepared for this to continue on in your name?"

Kora looked back at Gunnar. She could see the worry in his eyes. The villager near the bell in front of the longhouse held the hammer, ready to strike when she gave the order to do so. Her heart raced, but she knew what she must do. She motioned for the villager to lower the hammer. He paused then placed it on the ground. Kora turned back to Noble. He looked at her he as if he just claimed complete victory. "I thought not. Now say your goodbyes. Your father awaits, Arthelais."

Kora turned and walked towards Gunnar. She wrapped her arms around him. "What are you doing?" he pleaded in a hushed tone, not understanding what was happening as he hadn't heard the conversation with Noble. She shook her head. "I'm sorry. I cannot let this place die for me."

He tried to catch her gaze and touched her hand. "Kora, he's lying to you. I know you know this."

She met his gaze, holding back tears before embracing him tightly. "I know what I'm doing. Please let me go."

He held her. "I can't." His voice cracked as he said this in her ear. With one hand he pulled her gun from her holster and twisted his body away from her, straight towards the bell. He pulled the trigger. The shot, with perfect aim, sent the loud noise to signal for the battle to begin. The ring echoed through the silent village and valley. Noble's eyes grew large as his grin turned to a sneer. The soldiers behind him looked at each other in confusion. A layer of silence descended before chaos ensued. The burlap and dirt cover over the trench next to Noble's dropship was tossed to the side.

A villager stood poised to blast the ship with an anti-armor bazooka on his shoulder. Before the soldiers could stop him, he fired the weapon. The trench filled with the weapon's discharged smoke. Noble dove to the ground as his ship exploded upon impact, shrapnel shooting in all directions. He looked at the ground and made a fist. The explosion seemed to shake the village and made his head and ears throb. The shouting of his soldiers sounded like a distant echo from the ringing in his ears. He looked up to see the smoke clearing. However, the black vapor of his anger took hold of him. From his vantage point he could see the villager with the bazooka duck back into the trench.

Noble jumped to his feet, ignoring the bullets above his head and the fighting around him. He refused to be bested by peasants or a rogue assassin. With speed he leapt into the trench and pulled out his pistol. Without hesitation he unloaded one shot point blank into the head of each villager he found crowded in the trench. He looked at the body of one of them and the river of blood seeping from the wound in his forehead. His eyes caught a jagged-edged blade attached to the belt of the villager. He took it into his hands then turned towards the darkness of the trench. There had to be more of them.

Noble began to stomp down the narrow row. He could smell the wet soil. The scent flared his anger because this land and everything on it should be his for the taking without question. In front of him were two young farmers, reloading their weapons with nervous glances. Engrossed in their tasks, they didn't notice him stalking them from the dark recesses of the trench. It was obvious they were not seasoned soldiers, the way they fumbled with the weapons. Noble gripped the blade tighter.

"Reload!" shouted the taller farmer.

"You're all set, go!" said the other.

Before they could shoot, Noble rushed towards them. He plunged the blade into the side of the farmer with the rifle then pulled the blade out to stab him in the neck. The man dropped his weapon and slumped down dead. With his free hand, he smacked the other farmer across the face, breaking his nose. As the farmer cried out in pain and stumbled against the wall, Noble stabbed him in the belly with relentless fury. Blood sprayed across the trench.

"Pathetic," he spat under his breath. He stepped over their bodies with the intention to find as many villagers in hiding as possible before they could do more damage. Just ahead, a light illuminated the end of the trench. *That one…* he thought. It was the farmer with the bazooka who blew up his dropship. Noble licked his lips and moved towards the unsuspecting man, who had his back to Noble. His movements were swift and steps long to kill him before he had a chance to get another shot above ground. This was a battle he refused to lose. That bitch

Kora had to be taught a lesson. He relished the idea of seeing her face as she looked at the dead bodies of these inconsequential villagers she wanted to save so badly.

He wanted her to live through that before being executed. The pain and horror she would experience in that moment before death excited him. The excitement he felt in that moment was so intense that for a split second he thought of the Twins... the pleasure. How he would enjoy watching her be tortured on her knees. His steps quickened as the farmer moved to lift the bazooka and strike again. Noble thrust the blade into the back of his neck and the left side of his lower back. The bazooka slipped out of his hands before his body fell to the ground like rotten fruit from a tree.

Noble's lips curled to a smile. He could hear the battle waging above his head. Noble looked above the edge of the trench. Imperial soldiers continued to fire upon any villager in sight before jumping into trenches like the one he stood in. Now was his moment to run for his dropship.

"Go, Den! Now!" he heard an out-of-sight voice shout above the firefight. A large man he remembered from his first time here scrambled out of the trench. His massive body lurched forward with a burlap sack across one shoulder. He pulled out a grenade belt, letting the sack fall. His muscular arm flexed as it swung the belt towards the open bay doors of the dropship rising from the ground. Den began to sprint away. It didn't take long for the dropship to explode overhead. Den was thrown to the ground. Noble ducked into the trench to avoid the blast wave as it rumbled towards him. He stared at the dead bodies again and took a deep breath before climbing out of the trench and running for cover.

Den spotted the wicked admiral running towards a dropship and pushed himself off the ground to chase Noble across the field before he could escape. Den pumped his arms hard as he ran to catch up to Noble, wincing at the pain from his fall. The dropship ramp was within sight as Noble ran towards the open doors. With all his bulk and strength, Den leapt onto the ramp and tackled Noble. They crashed into the metal grating as the engines revved and roared to lift off. The wind whipped around the grappling men as they continued to rise off the ground with the bay doors still open. Den reached for his blade attached to his belt. His strength was matched by Noble, who held his own weapon still stained with the blood of the farmers. Despite being significantly larger than Noble, Den struggled with the newly modified admiral. His eyes searched for a weakness in the man. Noble grinned and shouted over the din of the engines. "You can't win this one without losing your life."

"If I don't kill you, Kora will. I know this. You are still just a man at the end of the day." Den took a swipe at Noble, catching him across the chest. Noble looked down at the torn cloth then charged towards Den with his blade out. The tip caught Den on his right arm and left side of his neck as Noble swung wildly but skillfully. Den matched his swings with his long reach. One blow slicing across Noble's right thigh. Noble

REBEL MOON

149

winced. Den used that moment of weakness to land a punch across his jaw, knocking Noble back towards the deck of the dropship.

Den was poised to go for the kill when Noble kicked him with the heel of his boot on the side of his knee. Den's knee buckled. Ready to return Den's favors, Noble cut Den's wrist and the forearm of the hand that held his blade. Den dropped the blade but didn't miss the incoming swipe towards his face. Den used his bare hands to wrap around Noble's neck. His eyes were wild as he squeezed to choke out the life of the man who wanted to destroy his home. Full of fury and focus, Den didn't see Noble's spiderlike fingers frantically clawing towards one of the fallen blades.

Den continued to squeeze, ignoring the pain of his wound, the pain of his fall. None of it mattered. The veins bulged from Den's neck, his face almost purple with rage, then his grip eased. He looked down at the blade thrust into his neck. His eyes went distant and lips opened, but before anything could escape, Noble slapped his hand across his mouth and pushed him backwards. Den remained still.

"I guess you will never know what happens to Kora. But I can't wait until she sees your carcass in the fields where it belongs."

Noble kicked Den's body until it tumbled off the ramp, twenty feet above the fields. He took a moment to look at the unmoving body and smiled. Den died better than most: he should thank Noble for that. Soldiers were overrunning the villagers trying to fight back. There would be nothing left of them at that rate. Noble was pleased with what he saw and rushed onto the main deck of the dropship to set a course for the Dreadnought. Next to him were two dropships, one of which smoked from a hit, but through a miracle of engineering was managing to make it back to the Dreadnought for repairs. It was a shame he couldn't get Arthelais. She would still be dead if they obliterated the village from space. That would have to be enough.

Kora and Gunnar jumped into the cold river when the first dropship, the one closest to them, exploded. She hadn't anticipated that. She was more than ready to give herself up. They found cover beneath the stone bridge. Kora blinked and shook her head with the sound of the explosion still ringing in her head.

"Are you alright?" Gunnar shouted over the sounds of ensuing battle.

She nodded as she wiped water from her face. "The granary!"

They trudged towards the bank farther down the river with bullets whizzing above their heads. With the way clear, they climbed out, keeping out of sight, and they ran crouched towards the back of the granary. There was a uraki tied and waiting. This was for Kora to reach her dropship according to the original plan. Gunnar untied the uraki and jumped on its back.

Kora paused, dripping wet and looking up at him. "Why did you stop me? He said he would have let you live."

Gunnar shook his head as he breathed hard. Water and sweat dripped on the uraki's neck. There was heat in his eyes, his teeth bared. "You know he would say anything to have you surrender without a fight. But his words are worthless. You're part of us now, part of me. And we won't let you sacrifice yourself to a lie. *I* won't."

Gunnar extended his hand as small explosions hit the ground near them. Kora didn't move or blink with the fight creeping closer to them. He continued to look her in the eyes. Kora could see—*feel*—the love he possessed for her. It was more frightening than the battle around them, but not having him in her life was scarier. She knew that. He continued to hold his hand out to her.

"Now let's go. We gotta get you up to that ship. You're our only chance."

Kora took his hand for him to lift her up onto the uraki. She mounted the beast behind him and wrapped her arms around his waist. As he moved the uraki into a gallop towards the hidden dropship, she rested her cheek against his back. She closed her eyes, hearing his heartbeat and feeling his breath. His body, his warmth made her feel safe despite the possibility of death with the horror of war on their doorstep. This was all she wanted. And if she died in that moment, with him beside her, then it was truly a life worth living after all her misdeeds and misjudgment.

They were moving fast when another explosion caused the uraki to reel. Gunnar's face was overcome with fear. Kora looked on. "It's a dropship. Good. We need to hurry and take advantage of this. Go!"

Gunnar heeled the uraki to move faster towards the waterfall and their own dropship. He didn't like the scene from the fields. He needed to be with his people on the ground.

Imperium soldiers began to advance on the interior of the village. They exchanged gunfire with the villagers, who relentlessly defended their positions from the ground and the trenches. The villagers were outnumbered as the soldiers stomped across the bridge like a virulent flesh-eating plague destroying soft tissue. They slowed down when they reached the village itself. All was quiet as they entered the courtyard and scanned their surroundings in confusion.

The soldiers looked in all directions, trying to search for any clues as to why they seemed to be alone. The only sound was that of the fight in the fields in the distance and their breaths. With the moment of pause, the soldiers were taken by surprise when the volley of shots fired at them from all fronts. They crouched for cover, automatically and indiscriminately returning fire.

"There!" The commander pointed beyond the village bell towards a large barricade made from odds and ends. Only the silhouettes of the makeshift fighters could be seen.

Tables, planks of wood, heaped sacks of grain appeared to be put together in haste. The commander sneered at the sight. "These idiots really think this will work. How pathetic. We go now! Spare no one!" he shouted.

The soldiers moved in unison, returning the gunfire. Splinters of wood and plumes of grain shot into the air as the battle intensified. A villager ran from behind the barricade towards cover. The soldiers watched the man scramble. "Look at the rat. Got 'em on the fucking run!" said one of them.

The commander rushed towards the barricade with his gun drawn and climbed over the deflating sacks of grain. At the top he stopped. His eyes wide as he scanned the ground. "The fuck…?" There were no villagers there, only simple scarecrows standing at attention. He grumbled, his face turning sour with acrimony as he turned to warn his soldiers of the trap.

Before he could open his mouth, a bullet hit him square in the face, knocking him backwards with a spray of blood. The soldiers moved in confusion without the certainty of their leader telling them what to do. A shower of bullets began to hit them from seen and unseen spaces.

"Fire back!" shouted one of the soldiers, trying to reorganize their regiment.

Bodies fell like swatted flies as a machine gun on the top of one of the tallest buildings closest to the center pounded the trapped soldiers with fire. As the soldiers begin to thin, more villagers jumped from their hiding spaces for the attack. Milius had perched themself in an attic of a building. They waited with sniper patience for soldiers to come into their crosshairs before pulling the trigger. Every aim resulted in more dead Imperium soldiers.

Titus ran out of the granary with his own group of villagers. They appeared less than ready compared to the heavily armored soldiers, yet he led them with pride. With his weapon raised, he shouted, "The time has come, for all that you love, for your home… protect each other and show them no mercy!"

His band of fighters roared with cheers and shouts as they charged towards the fight. Tarak emerged from the stables with twenty villagers armed only with scythes and farm equipment for weapons. He smiled seeing his brother in arms and shouted, "Can't let Titus and your brothers do all the work! Are you ready?"

The farmers following him shouted back with blades in the air, "To fight and die!"

"Let's leave the dying to your enemy. Follow me!" he shouted before charging towards the battle. The two groups began to merge as they caught a swarm of soldiers. Both Titus and Tarak met their opponents head on with blows and blades. Titus snatched a weapon from a soldier as he thrust a blade into his heart. Tarak wrangled a gun from a soldier, knocking him to the ground. The soldier pulled out a concealed weapon and aimed it towards Tarak. Tarak got his shots in before the soldier. With their immediate enemies dead, Titus nudged Tarak. Both men exchanged grins then ran farther into the heat of battle together.

REBEL MOON

155

. . .

Kora and Gunnar moved through the veil of water and into the cave. The sound of the waterfall filled the space, drowning out the fighting. They dismounted from the uraki. Gunnar led the uraki out the opposite side then followed Kora into the dropship. Kora whipped off her cloak. Gunnar looked at the bloody Imperium uniform she began to put on, then her newly shorn hair. "You look like one of them."

She looked down at the stained fabric. "I was. Not anymore. Now they bleed."

Gunnar pulled out an Imperium jacket from the saddlebag he'd brought. He looked at it with disgust before putting it on. He shrugged and pulled at the chest to adjust the fit. She glanced at him while preparing the ship as she sat at the control panel.

He nodded. "You sure this thing can fly?"

She cocked her head towards the seat next to her. "Hold on."

Gunnar scrambled for his seat whilst she pushed the throttle forward. The ship jolted to life then blasted through the waterfall.

"There," said Gunnar as he pointed towards the gap in the valley where the village lay. She guided the ship low across the ridgeline and hovered out of sight from the other dropships ascending towards *The King's Gaze*. One of them smoked as it trailed behind the others.

"What's next?" he asked.

"We drop into formation and hope they just take us in. When I give the signal, pull the pin and start the smoke."

Gunnar nodded and reached for the saddlebag. "I have the animal blood in the skin. We should dress in it." He splashed his hands and wiped them on her uniform over the previous stains. Kora glanced towards him before focusing on the controls again. The dropship eased into formation.

"My turn." She turned to him and took the skin. She soaked her hands with blood and saturated his uniform. Her fingers pressed more blood into the holes in the fabric. Gunnar watched her every move as she glanced up at him. With what was left on her fingers, she flicked on his face. They faced each other in uncertainty. Kora pulled him close and kissed him hard, blood smears on her own skin. She pulled away. "Blow the smoke."

Gunnar grabbed a smoke grenade from the saddle bag and rushed to the back of the ship. He pulled the pin then tossed it into a hatch. Gunnar sat next to Kora. They both watched for signs of smoke. When light plumes of smoke began to grow and cross the bridge window, they looked at each other.

"Hope the rest of it goes this smoothly," said Gunnar, breaking the tension as they neared the enemy. The other ships continued to cruise towards *The King's Gaze*. More smoke billowed from their ship.

"Looks like we have to go rogue here… look." Kora pointed to the damaged ships veering away from the others. The others included Noble. "We keep going. I'll handle this."

Kora guided the dropship into the docking bay, filling it with smoke. A voice screamed into the bridge. "That ship has taken damage!"

Kora flipped on her comms link. "Control, I have casualties and my controls are not responding... I'm surrendering control."

The docking officer sounded less perturbed. "We've got you, soldier. We're going to put you down into the main hangar for maintenance and medical extraction."

Kora flipped off the comms link. Gunnar whispered, "What now?"

"We wait and listen."

Gunnar took in what he could see from the cockpit. His eyes watched in horror at the power the Imperium possessed just from the air. "My god," he said to himself. Their ship moved deeper into the Dreadnought. It jerked when mechanical arms grabbed hold of it, and guided it closer. A coupling membrane extended towards the hatch and sealed around it. They continued to watch from the cockpit. Gunnar touched her arm and flicked his head towards the ship next to them. Noble marched down a ramp.

"Send the second wave now!" he shouted.

Kora and Gunnar looked at each other with fear for the village in their eyes. "We have to do this, no matter the cost," said Gunnar.

Dropships descended and landed on the upturned fields near the village. Ships and boots decimated the pristine land. Fresh soldiers piled out and prepared for another assault. On the other side of the river, the bulk of the remaining Imperium soldiers fought behind the burnt-out shell of an exploded dropship. They continued to fight hard against the villagers who gave them relentless hell. They all paused for a moment when the ground beneath their feet quaked as a gigantic beetle-like mech rose to four legs and stomped from the field towards the village.

The fresh Imperium soldiers used its substantial body for cover as they made their way to the heat of the battle and countered the villagers in the trenches. As the mech passed through the field, impervious to flying bullets and anything else thrown at it, Imperium soldiers jumped into the trenches with orders to kill on sight. Every villager charged with blind courage, desperate to salvage their home. They were overrun. There were more soldiers than village fighters and their pitchforks were no match for the sophisticated weapons of the Imperium that killed in an instant.

With robotic precision the Imperium soldiers overtook the trenches, soaking the soil in spilled blood. A young villager with only small hairs just above his lip groaned as he raised his head out of the dirt. Bloody dirt caked the side of his face and ear. Blood trickled from his nose. Soldiers charged past him, more occupied with the others fighting them. He crawled arm over arm, dragging his body and moaning with his face turning red from the exertion. Blood seeped from his side. He moved forward until he scratched at the dirt wall. When he hit the hidden panel, he tossed it to the side. This would be the end of him, but he had known this was a possibility. This would be a good death. Inside the panel was an explosive charge.

His hand trembled as he reached for it. With his hand barely touching the explosive, he closed his eyes and squeezed. Fire swelled and screams rang out through the trench like a blazing serpent as bombs along the dirt walls exploded. Imperial soldiers were incinerated and torn to shreds. Their blood became a smoky vapor settling over the fields. Yet still more soldiers stormed forward with orders to create carnage.

Titus and Tarak held their ground near the courtyard at the base of the bridge, fighting off the Imperial soldiers storming in from the fields. The two men gave each other cover while cutting down the ferocious tide from entering the village. They glanced up from the fight at a rumbling below their feet. The two stationary mechs rose to their feet and moved forward. The machine gun that cut the soldiers down in the trap turned to the mech. The hailstorm of bullets ricocheted against its thick metal exterior. It belched a single missile that destroyed the building. Debris and dust was hurled across the village. Soldiers and villagers on the ground ducked for cover as smoke filled the atmosphere with a heated haze that caused them to cough.

In the distance, Milius could see the building collapse to rubble. They shot at the mech until there was no ammunition left. Milius threw the weapon aside without looking at it. The mech reared its head towards the village bell. Milius shook their head in horror then ran into the granary. They searched the portion of the floor built over the river. The sound of rushing water was just behind a small trapdoor. Milius threw open the hatch and jumped into the river. The iciness gripped their body, but invigorated their resolve as it washed away the sweat and grime of battle. Milius swam hard against the current as bullets flew over their head. They ignored everything except the mech. The machine charged again and fired. The village bell that had rang for centuries was obliterated in seconds.

Milius scrambled, out of breath, up the bank of the river. They removed a blade from their sodden trousers upon seeing an Imperial soldier not far away. They ran across the field to catch the soldier by surprise. Milius yanked back the soldier's neck, slit his throat, then let loose a primal scream as the body fell to the ground, but a familiar rumbling caused them to look back. Another mech was on the move.

They looked around for cover, but all that was left of the field was ditches and craters. Milius jumped into one and waited while peering out. It advanced towards the bridge where Titus and Tarak fought with fury against the mounting odds. Imperial soldiers and village fighters resorted to hand-to-hand combat. Villagers wielded their sharpened scythes in bloody rage against the invaders.

The stones on the bridge were bathed in blood. Milius looked on, ready to join the fray when the machine was out of the way. As the mech passed, its giant steps shifted the ground. A discarded rocket launcher rolled out of the dust. Milius crawled towards the weapon and grabbed it as quickly as possible. They kneeled on one knee, took aim, then squeezed the trigger. "You can fuck right off, motherfucker."

The rocket whizzed through the air and hit the mech in the center of its body. The top of the machine exploded as its legs wobbled then buckled to the ground. Milius watched the smoking heap then ran towards the fight.

Kora and Gunnar took their staged positions in the cockpit. Five armed medics rushed in and placed a slumped-over Kora onto a gurney then lifted Gunnar up from the floor and placed him on a gurney, beside her. The lead medic punched in the medical bay on the side of the hovering gurney. They glided through the belly of *The King's Gaze* while their vitals were scanned for injuries. Large double elevator doors opened at the end of the hallway. The gurneys carrying Gunnar and Kora floated in.

The head medic had a puzzled look on his face as he glanced at the four other soldiers. "This is odd. I can't find a wound. How about that one? They stable?"

The other medic looked at the results. "Hmm. Pulse is low... but I don't..."

Kora's eyes snapped open. She grabbed the medic's face with both hands and headbutted him hard. He reeled back and fell to the ground. Before the others could react, she drew her weapon and shot all four of them. She turned from the bodies to the elevator controls. She pounded the panel, bringing it to a stop. The fallen medic held his nose and reached for his weapon, eyes straight on Kora. Gunnar jumped off the gurney, stomped on the hand of the medic, and then put a boot in his face. The medic didn't move again.

Kora looked back to Gunnar. "Give me your satchel charges."

Gunnar took off the charges stored in pouches slung across his chest and handed them to Kora. She secured them across her body then looked back at Gunnar. "Try and make your way back to the hangar. Find us a ship. We won't have long to get off this thing before it blows."

She turned to leave. Gunnar grabbed her arm and pulled her close despite being surrounded by death. "My turn." He kissed her with a passion that neither would ever forget. Their lips and tongues memorized each other's taste. The desire they possessed. His hands held her waist tightly. An alarm in the distance broke their moment, reminding them both they were on enemy turf and not lost in a field on the cusp of making love all night. He gazed into her eyes. "I'll be waiting."

She nodded and opened the elevator doors. She whipped around to look at Gunnar one last time but the doors had already closed. She faced an empty hallway and began to navigate through the maze of the Dreadnought. She found herself near the engine room when she heard approaching voices and footfalls. The crew spoke in hushed tones and walked quickly. She ducked into a dark, short hallway to avoid them.

When they were out of sight, she stepped back out to the hallway and towards the engine room. She kept her head down as five engine crews worked, deep in concentration. They monitored *The King's Gaze* and its energy levels. The room was washed in a light glow from the reactor monitors. She climbed a metal ladder that led to a catwalk above a few soldiers shoveling organic matter into two rows of six hot furnaces. She watched her steps as she peered below. The closer to the reactor, the brighter the light.

She squinted as she approached. At the far end of the catwalk was the heart, the power source of the Dreadnought. There stood the large statue in the shape of a bound humanoid on her knees. The Kali. Thick clear tubes emitting a white light snaked from its head. Energy surged from the statue directly into the walls. None of the workers noticed Kora as she slipped past in silence. She knew exactly where she needed to go to place the charges.

When close enough, Kora took out each explosive charge from the pouches slung across her body. They would activate once attached to the Kali, their timers set for seven minutes. The Kali's eyes snapped open when the charges were placed on her forehead. Kora stared back at her, reminded of the first time she had looked upon one. She sensed its sadness and pain. Feelings she knew all too well. But as a child, there was nothing she could do about it. Kora touched the face of the Kali and closed her eyes.

In her mind she could hear and feel her. The energy made her entire body tingle, and her mind went to a place as distant as dreams. She envisioned the Kali being set free at long last and rising from the floor with her bounds falling away. Her standing body could barely be contained in the room.

A voice that was not her own spoke in a calm and soothing tone. "It's all right, Kora. I know you don't want to kill me. But I also know it's the only way. So like Issa, I too forgive you. Because one day you will wake my sisters and their wrath will be my vengeance."

Kora opened her eyes and could see the Kali still looking at her. A single tear fell from the Kali's large open eye. When she turned to move, a voice shouted from the direction of the ladder. "You! You there… What are you…?"

Kora turned to see one of the crew standing at the end of the catwalk. He paused at her blood-spattered face and uniform. Her gaze filled with intention and hate. He began to walk towards her and draw his weapon when she rushed him. She kicked him between the legs then landed a blow across his face. As he reeled back, she unholstered her weapon and aimed. The clean shot caused his limp body to fall to the floor below. The soldiers working below looked up. Their eyes focused on Kora, who calculated her next moves.

Seven minutes, she thought to herself before jumping down. When she landed on her feet, she pulled out her gun and aimed it at the crew members ready to attack.

One tried to grab the satchel and choke her with the strap. She swung her body and elbowed him in the torso. When his grip slackened, she continued to twirl towards him and shot him in the neck. The commanding officer watched in disbelief as she exchanged punches with a second crew member. He looked at the statue then back at Kora before running to the main comms. He slammed his hand against the button. "Intruder alert! Repeat, intruder!"

Kora ignored the loud intercom and kicked one of the crew members who swung a pipe at her. She was nimble, avoiding his blows while waiting to get a clean shot. He raised the pipe and charged. She aimed and hit him directly through the chest three times. He fell with the pipe clattering to the ground.

Another voice shouted over the intercom in the engine room. "This is the communications officer. Sending backup. What is the nature and numbers of the intruders?"

He looked back and stammered as Kora stood over the final crew member with her boot on his chest as she unloaded one shot through his skull. "It's just one woman! Just one wom—"

Kora raised her gun and pulled the trigger. He fell on the controls with a gaping hole through the center of his forehead. Blood saturated the screen. She holstered her gun and ran to the exit. There was no time to spare before the explosives detonated.

· · ·

The communications officer on the main bridge attempted to reach the engine room again. There was only silence. Noble walked over to the seated officer and Cassius followed. "What was that?" asked Noble.

The comms officer looked confused as he continued to fiddle with the controls. "There is a situation in the engine room. He said a woman has infiltrated the ship."

Noble's eyes narrowed as if he could see exactly who it was and what she had done. "Arthelais is aboard the ship."

Cassius looked to Noble. "Sir... That's impossible."

His thin lips curled to a wicked smile. "No, it's her. Of course it's her. She's come to us. Alert all sectors. I want her captured at once."

Cassius gave Noble a nod. As he began to turn to fulfill his orders, Noble placed a hand on his shoulder. "And now, Cassius, you may target the village."

Cassius looked into Noble's black eyes. They possessed nothing behind them. He would kill anyone that stood in the way of this new mission of capturing his target. Noble had the scent of blood in his nose and the taste of it in his mouth. "Sir, the grain."

Noble gave him an incredulous look and leaned closer to Cassius' ear. "The Scargiver has come to us. We have no more need for the village. I would rather the men starve than risk exposing ourselves to another one of Titus' tricks."

Noble pulled back again with that sinister smile. Cassius could still feel his stale breath, a cold deathly wind in his ear. He had to say something because even this seemed a step too far for a single reward that would only benefit Noble. "But we have men on the ground."

Noble continued to stare at him with an evil glare. "A few less mouths to feed..."

Cassius and Noble held each other's gaze. "Now destroy it!" shouted Noble. Cassius knew this was the end of something. His dignity, perhaps his life. But he had his orders first. And he didn't want to die. Not yet. "You heard the admiral. Give the order!"

The Dreadnought officer at weapons control began her preparations. "Charge the cannons."

Cassius remained still whilst Noble walked away. He wondered how nothing haunted that man, because he knew he would have to live with the fact that he had sacrificed his own men, their lives, for his own and Noble's personal agenda. His sick climb to licking the regent's boots. Cassius would watch the destruction. He deserved that punishment.

Gunnar exited an elevator, rushing back to the hangar—to the best of his memory, anyway. Three officers approached at the end of the corridor. He didn't want a confrontation— not now they had made it this far. And there was no time to spare for a fight. He ducked into a deep doorway, hoping they wouldn't notice him. His heartbeat pounded in his ears as he tried to calm his breathing. He listened for their steps to come and hopefully go. But he heard much more.

"Hold. The second wave has been ordered to stand down. The admiral has decided to vaporize the village with our big guns here on *The King's Gaze*," said one of the officers.

"Really? I guess the rumors of taking the fugitives alive were just that."

Gunnar watched them walk away feeling an intense mixture of panic and fear at the world unraveling before his eyes. They were ready to fight Imperium soldiers to the last. They couldn't fight the cannons of a Dreadnought. Everyone and everything he knew, gone in seconds. He had to tell Kora. He peeked around the corner to see if anyone else approached. No one. He pulled out his comms. Panic began to grip his entire body. There would be no hiding it. "Kora! Kora! Noble is turning the guns towards the surface. He doesn't give a shit about the grain. He wants the village destroyed."

There was a pause. "The charges are set. I have about four and a half minutes."

"For what?"

"Just have the ship ready."

Gunnar peeked out of his hiding spot again to make sure it was clear. Four and half minutes wasn't a long time. He prayed for a miracle.

FROM INSIDE THE LONGHOUSE THE BATTLE COULD ONLY BE HEARD. THAT WAS enough. The villagers looked at the walls, fearing they would fall on their heads, or be blasted through with some Imperium weapon. The children remained close to their parents. Nemesis stood tall and calm with them behind her. She had been waiting to spring into action if the time came. That time had arrived. A booming voice shouted at the other end while banging on the blockaded doors. "This is the Krypteian Guard. We are coming in, whether you like it or not!"

The villagers shuddered with every crack and bang of the wood. Children whimpered. Nemesis stood in a wide stance with both blades poised to slice open the intruders. A guard shouted, "Now!" The front doors ripped open.

Five Krypteia stood before Nemesis. Their faces were devoid of mercy or care and they were armed with weapons the villagers in the longhouse could not compete with. The time for strategy was gone. Nemesis charged towards them with the intention of killing them all. They raised their weapons and began shooting in her direction. She deflected their bullets, her swords tearing through the air. One of the guards took three swipes at her, all three times she caught his blows. Sparks flew as metal hit metal. When the others attempted to bypass her to get to the villagers, she swung her body and swords, creating her own blockade.

A guard attempted to grab her left metal hand. She lifted her arm and thrust her right sword through his heart. Blood spurted across her face when she pulled out her sword. Two others approached her from opposite sides. Nemesis twisted both blades to prevent them from having a clear shot or being able to get close to her. The largest guard moved with the heaviness of an uraki. Not as foolhardy or nervous as the other guard, he held back with another guard, observing the cornered villagers. His eyes landed on Aris and Sam, who protected a few of the children without parents.

The bigger kids held the little ones, who were covering their ears and eyes. The larger guard elbowed the one next to him and cocked his head towards them. Sam stepped forward with her loaded blunderbuss. Looking him in the eye with spite and hatred, Sam aimed and pulled the trigger without hesitation. The guard was thrown back by the bullet that ripped a hole through his chest. Blood oozed from the wound and onto the floor. The large guard gave Sam a menacing glare and rushed towards her. Sam stumbled back to reload her weapon. Her fingers trembled.

Aris turned from the children to see the juggernaut bearing down on Sam. He leapt to intercept the giant then stopped in horror. He recognized that face. The guard standing before him was one of the men who had helped slaughter his family. Aris tightened his grip on the blade in his hand and screamed with fury until the veins on his neck bulged. "You!" he shouted to the guard, who didn't recognize him. One kill was the same as the other.

He opened his arms to welcome the fight from Aris, who sliced the air with his blade whilst careening towards the guard.

"You're a feisty kid," taunted the hulking soldier. He balled a fist and threw a punch at Aris, too slow. Aris ducked and sliced his unarmored thigh. The guard growled and gave Aris an uppercut. Enraged, Aris didn't back down when he stumbled back or notice the pain, instead regaining his footing and charging forward with his blade overhead in one hand. The guard pulled out his own blade ready to strike Aris. The young man brought the blade down and sliced deep into the inner forearm of the guard. The lumbering oaf screamed out from the pain and his grip loosened.

Aris pushed him to the ground with his entire body weight. The guard dropped his blade but grabbed the sides of Aris' arms to prevent him from plunging the blade into his neck. Aris tore his arms away from the man's grasp and punched him in the side of the head. This only enraged the guard, who shook off the blow and headbutted Aris in the mouth and chin. Blood spewed from his split lip.

As the guard scrambled to grab his blade again, Aris drove his farming blade into the center of his palm and then continued to punch him in the side of the head with his other hand whilst screaming. He pulled the blade out of the guard's hand and stabbed him through the throat. Without mercy or direction, Aris gripped the hilt with both hands and plunged the blade into any exposed flesh on the guard. His body and arms moved in an energetic frenzy despite the guard's dead and still body.

Blood and chunks of flesh slapped against Aris' body and face. He couldn't hear the children crying. Aris' entire body shook as Sam embraced him. His arms dropped at her touch.

"I'm here!" she said as she tried to comfort him. The blood on his hands and arms smeared across her tunic and sleeves as he clung to her. "I'm here. I'm here."

"I got him. That bastard… I got him for *them*… for my father," said Aris.

"You did. Now it's time to let go. We aren't done with this fight." He looked into her eyes and nodded and rose to his feet. He could hear the fight outside still raging.

Titus held the bridge with Tarak as best he could. Blood and dirt caked his body as he tossed a dead Imperium soldier over the bridge. Tarak pounded one foot into the skull of another. He held an axe in one hand and a hammer in the other. The two men exchanged glances as the bridge was clear for a moment. But beyond the village and in the fields, more soldiers were advancing.

"There!" shouted Tarak, his body tense again. He pointed towards Milius: they couldn't run towards the village due to a constant storm of bullets flying over their heads and hitting the ground where they had taken cover. Tarak was on the verge of running to help their fellow warrior.

Titus gave him a wary look. "No…" Tarak shot him a look of defiance. "I'm going."

"You can't help them!" Titus shouted back.

Tarak looked back at a crouching Milius. "From here I can't." Titus grabbed his forearm. "The enemy wants to draw us out. We must fall back and regroup."

Tarak pointed to Titus' weapon. "You can cover me with this or cover me with dirt. The choice is yours, General."

Titus took the weapon with reluctance. "When this is all over…"

Tarak nodded and gave him a half smile. "You can teach me that song you were singing the other night."

Tarak turned to run towards the fields and Milius when a boom and crack in the sky made them both duck. A small stone building exploded nearby, sending sharp shards of rock shooting through the air. Titus whipped his head towards Tarak. "Go! Hurry!" He aimed his weapon and began to shoot a clear way for Tarak to head into the fields. Soldiers began to make their way onto the bridge. Titus met the small band head on.

REBEL MOON

175

He aimed at the leader of the soldiers charging the bridge and hit him in the chest and neck. The soldier fell backwards, knocking into another close behind. The soldier stumbled but managed to hit Titus across the face with his rifle. Blood flew from his mouth, further enraging him. He matched the soldier's blow with a back hand across his face, then ripped the rifle from his hand. He buried the gun in the soldier's belly. The soldier fell dead.

Two soldiers attempted to surround him and grapple him to the ground. One of them aimed a gun towards his head. Titus ducked and the bullet lodged into the chest of the Imperium soldier behind him. He used the opportunity to pull the soldier closer to him by his armor. With both hands he gripped the man's helmeted head and twisted his neck. The soldier fell like a tree branch struck by lightning. Titus stood over his dead opponents with a sad mania in his eye. This was war.

He looked up to see a soldier stomping towards Milius, who reloaded their weapon. The soldier raised his arm but didn't get the opportunity to make the kill. Tarak grabbed a blade from his waist and slashed the soldier's neck. Blood ran down his chest and formed a pool in front of a wild-eyed Milius. Tarak extended his hand. "Let's go! We need to regroup!" Milius took his hand. They both sprinted towards the bridge and Titus.

"Incoming!" shouted Titus with his finger pointed behind them. A mech launched a missile in their direction.

The blast threw them off their feet. Before it could find

them again, they scrambled towards one of the trenches that had been heavily bombarded. Milius looked towards Tarak. "I would have done the same for you."

Tarak nodded. "I know. Now let's get out of here alive."

They moved to the edge and peered over. Another mech was on the move and headed in their direction. From the opposite side of the bridge they heard a shout. "Look!"

They followed the direction of the shouting and looked towards the sky. *The King's Gaze* hovered overhead with its cannons moving into position. That position was straight at them. "They are targeting the village!" shouted Titus.

"Fuck me…" Milius looked on in terror as the cannons aimed at them. "This couldn't all be for nothing."

"It's not over. Look."

The mech approaching them kicked up dirt and dust. They squinted and shielded their faces but could still see the twenty Imperium soldiers trailing behind it. In the distance, more dropships whizzed through the air and landed at the far end of the fields with more soldiers marching out in ant trails. There were more than they could handle. Tarak spotted a weapon and ammunition on the ground and picked it up.

Milius slumped into the trench with their head hanging. "This can't be it. Not again. How will they ever be stopped?"

"I don't know, but we don't have time to think about it!" A mech fired straight at them, blasting a hole next to the trench. The crater left them exposed and full of mud as they were tossed against the wall. With plumes of dust giving them some cover, they clawed out of the trench and ran towards a fallen mech. Bullets pierced the air next to them. Once behind the mech there was no other place to run that didn't put them in the line of fire. Both Tarak and Milius reloaded their weapons. Tarak looked up to the sky. "I thought to die in battle was all I wanted. Fighting for something."

Milius placed their hand on his shoulder. "Beside good men."

Tarak scanned the field filled with bodies and smoke. A shadow covered his face. "I think I was wrong. I don't want to die at all. But if I must…" Tarak extended his hand to Milius.

Milius took Tarak's hand with a smile. "Together."

Part of *The King's Gaze*'s lethal magnificence was its main weapon—the Sword of the King. The inside of the gun turret was small. The gunnery crew worked to carry out their new orders. A window with the width of ten feet and height of two feet at the front gave them a view of their target. The soldier in charge of loading the guns called out to the one who controlled them, "The gun is charged and ready to fire!"

The shooter nodded and turned to the control. He took them in hand and pushed them forward with the same emotions as a robot. The guns lowered into position.

He glanced at the screen showing a holographic image of

the village, the target. Heat signatures guided the shooter towards the clusters of people. The gunnery commander, just as stern as the crew, looked over the shooter's shoulder. "Are you ready?" she asked.

"Target acquired."

"Fire at will."

Shooting and shouts just beyond the door made them both turn. The door swung open with Kora's boot still in the air from kicking it open. Behind her a trail of bodies lay on the ground. The shooter's eyes widened with surprise.

"Do it!" screamed the commander.

Just as the gunnery crew member was about to pull the trigger, Kora unloaded her weapon into his head. His body slumped into his chair and his head thudded onto the controls. The commander glared at Kora as she reached for her weapon. With perfect aim she shot the commander three times in the chest and killed the rest of the crew. She tossed the corpse of the shooter out of the chair and took the controls. Her target was clear—the conning tower. The tower had to be destroyed to truly obliterate *The King's Gaze*. She would turn their own hateful stare back onto them.

Noble and Cassius stood inside the conning tower, waiting to see the destruction of Veldt. "What is the meaning of this?"

Cassius followed Noble's gaze. The turrets had swiveled towards them, making the conning tower the target. Cassius rushed towards the communications officer.

"What the hell is he doing? Find out what the hell is going on."

"Yes, sir." The officer flipped on his comms. "Sword of the King. What is your current status?"

There was no response. Noble stared at the turrets, knowing exactly what was happening and who was responsible. He had to act fast. "Don't bother…" he said under his breath before turning to sprint towards the elevator. Without any word of warning he shoved past Cassius, who watched the man he had served with unwavering loyalty abandon him like an off-world commoner, then looked back at the turrets that did not stop moving in their direction. Cassius turned to run towards the elevators. The rest of the crew stood to watch the turrets and the running Noble. Raised voices were followed by a stampede for the elevators. Noble stood in the center when Cassius reached the doors. His eyes were glassy with fear and desperation. He tried to pry them open with his hands. "Sir…" Noble took out his gun and shot Cassius in the face. He fell and the doors slammed closed.

Kora watched the entire tower explode in a fountain of fire and smoke. She watched the debris fall with a strange numbness. She prayed it was enough and that Noble was part of the shattered pieces in freefall. However, relief would only come when she knew for sure Noble had been vanquished for good.

● ● ●

The expectation of doom filled the entire village with dread. It was the end of all things when the turrets reared their guns. The blasts pumped straight for the village, but instead of the center, they hit the wave of Imperium soldiers at the edge of the field. The impact rippled against the soil like a drop of rain in a pond. Imperium soldiers and dropships were destroyed within moments. Clouds of dust filled the air and covered everything. In the thick of the smoke and dirt, everything seemed to stand still. Milius and Tarak coughed and rubbed their eyes. "I don't know what the hell just happened... you think they are all wiped out?"

Tarak squinted then his face dropped. "No... fucking unbelievable."

As the destruction settled, the faint outline of one mech still standing could be seen. There were also at least a dozen Imperium soldiers recovering from the blast. Tarak grabbed Milius' arm. "We better run. Looks like it sees us." The mech aimed its cannons towards the two.

"What is..." Milius pointed to another shadow emerging from the dust. It sounded like another machine coming to life with the whirring of gears and clicks. It was Jimmy. But not as he was when he took his first step on Veldt. His cape blew behind him. His faceplate had smears of war paint. In his hand he held a sharpened elk antler. He ran straight into the midst of the remaining Imperium soldiers. They fired their weapons towards him but his metal exterior withstood their bullets. He raised his weapon made of antler and cut them down one by one, with the ferocity of a wild beast of the forest but the precision of a machine. Jimmy had awakened and transformed into something completely new. Limbs, intestines, blood and chunks of flesh littered the ground and fell in his wake. Cries from the wounded echoed in the dusty air.

Milius and Tarak smiled as they watched on with disbelief. Tarak nudged Milius. "We should join in the fun."

Milius smirked and raised their weapon. Both fighters began to snipe the soldiers from the dead mech they hid behind. The Imperium soldiers looked in all directions, not knowing where the attack would come from. In no time at all, they were all dead from a bullet or the tip of a sharp antler. The only thing left standing was the mech. It turned to Jimmy, ready to fire. He leapt towards the cannons and aimed them towards the ground. The impact put a crater into the dirt but ripped one of his arms off in the process. It flew across the field. Jimmy continued to climb onto the mech. At the top, he ripped open the sealed metal manhole with the ease of breaking a man's neck. Jimmy disappeared inside.

The two soldiers manning the mech turned in surprise to see a faceless machine with glowing eyes staring them down. Jimmy thrust the antler up through the bottom of the face and mouth of the soldier at the controls. His eyes rolled back to only white as blood poured from the wounds. The second soldier fumbled with her weapon and attempted to aim it at Jimmy. She wasn't quick enough.

Jimmy pulled the pin from a grenade attached to the soldier's chest. "No! No! No!" she screamed as she tried to pull the grenade vest off. Jimmy leaped out of the mech and back onto the ground. Within seconds the metal war machine burst into flames, sending hot debris across the field. Jimmy stood tall and watched the destruction. Tarak hollered in joy at this sight and slapped Milius across the back. "Maybe there is hope for us yet."

Like everyone, Nemesis could feel the fighting outside as the bombardment shook the ground beneath her feet. Two Krypteia charged towards her with blades out. She caught one with her sword then screamed out in pain. The other sliced his blade across her back. As her torso arched, the guard in front of her brought down his blade and severed her hand. Her eyes burned with fury at this assault.

She ignored her wound and thrust her remaining sword into his belly. She pulled it out with enough time to swing around and catch the other guard across the chest. As she moved to strike again, the guard spun away then drove his blade straight into her chest.

Her mouth opened as her breath caught in her throat. Little Eljun screamed at seeing his hero cut down. He broke away from the other children with his own blade in hand. As fast as his young legs could move, he ran across the longhouse. He stabbed the guard in his side just below the ribs. The guard looked to Eljun, perturbed and without mercy. The little boy matched his scowl and twisted the blade, causing the guard to cry out. Eljun pulled out his weapon. Blood shot out of the wound, spraying his face. He raised his blade again and stabbed the guard. Nemesis could only watch as blood poured from her mouth. The guard grabbed Eljun by the throat and lifted him off the ground. His small feet kicked as he gasped for air like a little fish tossed out of water. His face began to turn blue.

"You little shit. I'll kill you too!" groaned the guard.

Nemesis kept her eyes on Eljun, his body beginning to slow as the guard tightened his grip on the boy's neck. Nemesis allowed the guard's blade to sink deeper into her body to get closer to Eljun. With the last of her strength she pulled the blade from the guard's side and slit his throat. A sheet of blood poured from his neck and he dropped Eljun. He fell to the ground in a coughing fit, regaining his breath. With the last guard now dead, the villagers in the longhouse rushed to the aid of Nemesis and Eljun.

The crying little boy crawled towards Nemesis. Her eyes were weary slits as she clung to the last minutes of life. "Be still my child, you fought with honor." She reached behind her neck with her one hand, unclasped the necklace that once belonged to her daughter, and pressed it into his bloody hand. "This is yours now. Always fight with honor." He nodded as she gazed into his eyes until her life ended with a final act of love and comfort.

In the distance, in the fields, a cloud of dust filled the air. A moment later the sky rumbled. Through the clouds. large pieces of metal, pieces of the Dreadnought's conning tower, began to fall to the ground. The village erupted in cheers.

Not far away, Titus shouted, "That's Kora!" It was the first display that gave him hope for a victory. "May you kill them all and make it back," he said to himself as he watched the sky.

KORA STILL MOVED ON BORROWED TIME. SHE HAD TO GET OFF THE SHIP. AS SHE rose from the seat, she aimed her gun at the turret controls, blasted them to pieces, then rushed for the doors. She ran down the corridor and made it to the elevator on the opposite side. Her comms switched on.

"Kora, where are you? It's less than a minute until the reactor blows." It was Gunnar.

"I'm almost to you."

The elevator stopped. The doors opened to reveal Krypteian Guards. Kora knew they wouldn't let her leave. They were twice her size and holding their swords. Kora fixed her gaze upon them. Undeterred, she ran towards them, pulling the trigger in quick succession. She drove her body into a guard running towards her. Her right hand grabbed hold of the arm holding his weapon. She spun him around to use him as a shield from the other two. As their weapons discharged into their fellow soldier, she kneeled and aimed for their legs and torsos. Both fell at the same time.

One of them took two large strides towards her and swung his glowing blue sword in her direction. She ducked with enough time to position her gun beneath his chin and pulled the trigger once more. Red mist launched from the crown of his head. He fell at her feet. Kora looked at the sword glinting in the light. It still vibrated with scorching heat and energy, buzzing sharply. She pried it from his hand and walked back to the elevator. It burned her palm as she held it. She ripped a piece of cloth from a dead guard and wrapped it around her hand. She felt the weight of it as she twisted and turned it. She holstered her gun, satisfied with the sword, and directed the elevator to the hangar.

The elevator stopped and the doors opened. Kora paused. Noble stood before her, a Krypteian sword in one hand and a pistol in the other. Just behind him, about thirty yards away, was Gunnar and her way out. Noble glared at her while pointing the sword directly at her. "You're surrounded."

She took slow steps farther into the hangar. In her periphery she could see two Imperial soldiers on either side of her, but her eyes never strayed from Noble. He flashed her a wry smile as he walked closer to her. "Lay down your weapons."

Kora removed her weapons holster, but kept a tight grip on the sword. He looked at her with smug satisfaction as he moved closer to her. "I suppose I owe you thanks for not accepting my offer of surrender. Makes a better ballad if I slay you in combat. It was a good try—better than could have been expected from a bunch of weary farmers. Yet, you must know this ship can operate without a bridge."

She held his gaze, expressionless, as she waited for the explosives attached to the Kali to detonate. His eyes wavered for a moment as he searched her face, not knowing why she remained calm. Then a series of pops and deafening explosions echoed through the cavernous hangar. The room shuddered as the floor moved beneath their feet. He looked at her in shock as he stumbled back.

"But can it operate without its engines?"

Noble's eyes widened hearing this. He moved to attack. Two shots rang out nearby. The two guards on either side of Kora fell to the ground. Noble and Kora looked around at where the shots had come from. Gunnar stood behind Noble with his weapon drawn. Kora looked to Gunnar, then Noble, who raised his pistol towards Gunnar. She moved swiftly to attack Noble. She wouldn't get to him in time, but maybe she could throw him off, stop him from getting a clean shot. To no avail. Noble pulled the trigger. Bright red blooms appeared on Gunnar's chest as he fell to the floor.

"Gunnar!" Kora screamed as she renewed her assault on Noble. She hit Noble's arm–the one holding the pistol—with the butt of her sword. He dropped the pistol and jumped away before she got the chance to strike him with her sword. They circled each other with glowing blue blades in hand, trying to maintain their balance as the ship teetered, the ground becoming more and more unstable by the second. The Dreadnought's nose began to shift towards Veldt. The floor tilted and parts broke away, causing them to keep moving else they would slide off.

Gunnar's limp body tumbled and hit the wall, leaving a bloody trail from the gunshot. As the ship continued to spiral, the floor became the wall. Kora's and Noble's swords clashed with the echo of ten. She pushed hard to knock his out of his hand, or land a clean lethal cut, but his skill and strength had increased since they last fought.

"You just won't give up, Arthelais. I can see why you were once the darling of Balisarius," said Noble.

"No, I won't give up until you are dead!" Kora pressed forward as the ship rotated again and they fought on what was once the ceiling. Loose items clattered around them, alarms blared. It wouldn't be long until the Dreadnought broke apart and hit the ground. Noble gritted his teeth as he swung his sword with controlled hysteria. His only intention was to see her bleed and die.

He raised his sword and swung it again as Kora fought to keep her footing. Her blade slipped from her hands and fell to the ground. Knowing her only chance was to use the unsteady ground, she waited a beat until Noble moved with the rotation, to twist her body to use her elbow and upper arm to strike him across the jaw.

Noble flew back and fell to the ground from the blow. She looked around for her weapon. It was sliding across the floor towards a semi-conscious Gunnar. With eyes narrowed to slits and the deep wound to his chest still weeping blood, he caught the sword. Noble scrambled to his feet and punched Kora hard in the belly. The ship rocked and twisted as it burned through the atmosphere, heading for a collision with Veldt. She bowled over for a moment then grabbed his head with both hands as they fell to the trembling ground.

She pounded his head hard against the floor. He managed to grab her by the torso with his feet and legs then launched her over his head. She smashed into the ground. As she tried to get back up, Noble rose to his feet and picked her up in a chokehold. He tightened his arm around her neck as her hands clawed at his arms. Her mouth opened and eyes rolled back. He looked down on her red face with a sinister gleeful smile. "See. This could only end one way."

So consumed with murder, he didn't see Gunnar heave himself off the floor, her sword in his hand as he dragged it towards Noble. Blood spurted from his mouth with every step.

"Goodbye, Arthelais. I hope you enjoy—" Noble's arm slackened and he looked down. Kora's sword emerged from his chest. Kora fell from his grasp. Weak croaks escaped his lips as he touched the edge of the blade. Gunnar lifted his leg as if it weighed a ton and kicked him to the ground. Noble lay there, watching the ship fall to pieces before his very eyes. Kora took the blade and made sure he would never see anything ever again, beheading him.

Kora crawled towards Gunnar, who had collapsed from his wound. *The King's Gaze* was breaking apart. There were shouts from crew trying to escape and screams from those being crushed. Large pieces of machinery fell from every direction and flew through the air as the ship spiraled faster towards the planet. Crew who managed to make their way into a dropship flew out of the bays.

Kora looked at Gunnar's wounds, then into his eyes that struggled to remain open. "I'll die with you," she said to him with tears in her eyes. She stroked his face and kissed his lips when the floor beneath them shook. She whipped her head to the right to see a dropship had come loose and slammed next to them. She looked back to Gunnar and jumped to her feet, dragging him towards the dropship. She pulled him inside and ran to the pilot's chair. Kora pressed hard on the controls and zoomed out of the hangar. The dropship rocked violently. Their dropship was hit by debris and began to spin out of control.

She grabbed the controls to stop the ship from careening into the ground and bursting into flames. She had to land this thing the best she could. Gunnar needed help, and fast. As it approached the village, she pulled hard on the throttle. Smoke fogged the windows from the damage to the exterior. The ship skipped across the burned and cratered field. She glanced at Gunnar as they bounced against the ground. It finally came to a stop near the bridge. Kora rushed from her seat and slammed the control to open the doors. She pulled Gunnar out, hoping it wasn't too late. They had made it this far. *The King's Gaze* and Noble were both destroyed for good as the Dreadnought broke apart in the sky.

Kora cradled a dying Gunnar in her arms. She touched his face and tried to keep him awake. Tears clung to the bottom of her eyes and fell down, joining the dirt and blood staining her cheeks. "No. No you don't. Don't you dare die on me! I've got a future here, and I need it to be with you."

He smiled with a blood-coated mouth and touched her tears, wiping them away. "You've got a future alright. You live it for the both of us. Promise me."

She shook her head, still crying. "Dammit, I want you. I've lived my whole life doing as I was told, what was asked of me. I'm tired of it. I want you alive. Why can't I have this one thing?! Just this one thing!"

Kora began to sob and shake her head. She looked to the sky to see the escaped dropships in attack formation. Gunnar coughed up blood. His chest convulsed. She turned her attention back to him, her tears falling onto his hand, holding hers.

"Look what you did. You saved us. You saved all of us. I love you… but not for what you have done, but who *you* are. You are a light in the dark. Never forget that."

She continued to sob, the pain greater than any physical torture she could be subjected to. She opened her mouth to speak, but her words remained choked sobs lodged in her throat. He squeezed her hand the best he could and his voice reduced to a dry whisper. "It's okay… you don't have to say it back… I know what you are… and I love you."

She opened her lips again to speak when ships roared overhead. Dust and dirt circled around them. She looked up, expecting this to be the end, but they weren't Imperial ships. They were unmarked vessels strafing what was left of the Imperial soldiers on the ground. Cheers erupted from behind her. Titus, Tarak, and Milius punched the air with their fists at this unseen ally. Aris stood next to Sam with his arm around her. His eyes were wide with disbelief and tears.

The villagers emerged from their stations and hiding places to watch this new battle being waged. The Imperial dropships poised to attack the village became engaged in an aerial dogfight and were blasted from the sky one by one. They scattered, trying to avoid these new opponents, but didn't get far. One of the unmarked ships broke away and landed in the field. Devra Bloodaxe leapt out of the cockpit with a sword in one hand and a gun in the other.

Fresh for a fight, she stormed towards the Imperial soldiers approaching the village. With her gun raised she picked off the easy targets. Soldiers rushing towards her were met with her sword slashing indiscriminately across their bodies. She used both her weapons in tandem without missing a beat. Within minutes she was covered in blood and mud. One of the soldiers knocked her to the ground. Before he could set upon her, she swiped her sword just below his knees and removed both legs. He fell to the ground screaming in agony. She rose from the dirt and shot him between the eyes. Behind her, rebel ships aimed at the soldiers from the sky, sending them into the air and to their instant death.

Kora's body shook with relief. "Look, it's Devra Bloodaxe and the whole rebel fleet. It's… it's really over." No response came from Gunnar. She looked down to see his sky-blue eyes wide open, but no heartbeat or breath. Kora closed her eyes and grit her teeth as she pulled him closer. His head rested against her chest. "I love you. I love you, Gunnar."

She looked back up to the burning fields of Veldt and the rising smoke. The cost of rebellion is always loss. The legacy is freedom and dignity.

The sunset matched the crimson-stained soil of Veldt. A large funeral pyre blazed. In the center stood a pike with the flags of the fallen. Smoke rose like a pillar candle into the air. Hagen stood front and center before the flames next to Kora and Milius.

"From other worlds they came to fight for us… to die for us. From Byeol, Nemesis. From our own lands, Den and Gunnar. All displaying bravery heretofore unknown. To the lives lost here. To the lives lost on other worlds. To all those who refused to bend the knee to the Motherworld… may they find their peace."

Hagen's voice cracked as tears streamed from his eyes and the flames crawled up the pikes, consuming the flags Sam had lovingly made with her own hands as a tribute to the bravery of the warriors. Hagen cleared his throat and continued his speech. "We honor them now in the only way we can. By remembering their names when next we bring in the harvest. A season from now, a hundred seasons from now..." he paused to wipe his nose and eyes, "...and by carrying on. By carrying on."

Eljun bowed his head to cry as he clasped the necklace around his neck. Sam stood next to him with her head resting against Aris' shoulder. The entire village stood in respect for the dead who fought to protect their village. Above the longhouse, the banners of the remaining fighters blew in the breeze.

They all stood in front of the village bridge. Kora wore Gunnar's jacket and stared with vacant eyes into the flames. Nemesis' swords sparked in the flames as they were consumed with her body. Devra turned to Kora. "I am sorry. My brother was right. He always was."

Kora looked into her eyes. "When it mattered, you came."

"No. Not when it mattered. Not soon enough. I have much to learn about bravery from the lot of you." Devra turned to Milius and placed a hand on their shoulder. "Perhaps you most of all. You who showed strength when we did not. All of you honor the fallen."

Kora continued to look at the flames. A single tear slid down her cheek. Her entire face showed emotions she had masked through the fight. "Do not speak of me when you speak of honor and bravery. I lied to you… to all of you… Titus."

She turned to the general. His eyes were filled with compassion and his lips a soft smile. " I know, child."

"You know I am Arthelais, adopted daughter of the regent Balisarius and assassin of Princess Issa?"

His eyes twinkled in the firelight. "I know your name, yes. But you were not her assassin."

Kora searched his face. She looked at him in confusion.

"For the princess is still alive," he said.

She shook her head. "But I…"

He gave her an amused smile. "You thought she could be killed so easily? No… she's more than that."

Kora's lips quivered. She closed her eyes and opened them again. Her mind swirled with images of the past. "What am I to do?"

"You have a reason now, do you not? To find her and to fight."

Kora touched her weapon.

"If you do choose to fight, I will stand with you," said Devra.

Kora gave her a nod. Milius glanced towards Tarak, who also nodded his head in agreement. "All of us."

"And I as well," said Titus.

Kora looked at him with deep gratitude. "Thank you, Titus."

Tarak chimed in, "That's *our* General Titus."

They looked up to mechanical stomping. "If I can be of use…" Jimmy approached them. He held up a bloodstained antler. "I do have this. It is a most useful weapon."

Tarak chuckled and slapped him on the back. "You wish to fight with us, robot, and find this lost princess?"

"If what you say is true and the princess lives… I have no choice. I serve the line of the slain king. It is my honor to fight."

Kora looked above their heads at the glowing embers and ash being carried on the wind towards the sky. They looked like distant stars floating in the vast universe. She turned back to the crumbling pyre. There was nothing left here on Veldt for her but memory. "Yes, to find her and to fight."

A young girl no more than ten years old stepped forward. She took a deep breath and began to sing.

From far my home land calls to me
Over ever-rolling fields my heart is taken out of me
Fire within fire I follow your feet
Fire within fire my end will I meet
From far I hear my homeland cry
Under ever-gloaming skies thunder
Rolls up on her sighs
Fire within fire I follow your feet
Fire within fire my end will I meet
Far from far your wandering soul
Under stars I will never hold
Stars I will never hold
Must I let you go far from far my heart my home

No one spoke, only listened with tears streaming from their eyes as the bonfire consumed the bodies of the dead and the banners hanging above their bodies, with embers and smoke rising to meet the night.

Balisarius stood beneath a two-story stained-glass window, half dressed. Colored light filtered in from the grand window as he stared at the gray walls with his chest out and chin held high. Attendants worked to dress him in the highest ceremonial royal attire. A tunic was pulled over his head followed by the heavy cape embroidered with gold. His attaché walked with quick steps and a look of worry across his face. He swallowed hard when he stood before Balisarius. "Sire."

Balisarius glanced at him and held out a finger. "One moment. I do love this part."

He bowed his head for a laurel of gold leaves to be placed on his head. He closed his eyes, relishing every second of being treated like and believing he was the most important man in the universe. When the laurel was secured on his head, his lips curled to a smile. He straightened and opened his eyes. He stood like a king. His eyes glanced towards the attaché. "Tell me as we walk."

Balisarius moved from his attendants towards the doors. His footsteps hit the gleaming marble floor. A dozen guards and generals waited outside the doors and followed him as they walked down a corridor. The attaché scurried to keep in pace with him.

"You've brought word from Admiral Noble. When can we expect his return?"

The attaché stammered. "Yes… Well… We felt you should know as soon as we could confirm that we have no contact with the admiral and fear *The King's Gaze* is lost." The attaché held his breath for a beat after giving Balisarius this news.

Balisarius stopped before a doorway. He furrowed his brow. "Lost?"

The attaché looked towards the stony-faced soldiers and to the floor. "Destroyed, sire."

"What?" The sternness in Balisarius' voice echoed through the archway of the high ceiling hall.

"We were able to confirm that the ship disintegrated upon impact with the moon Veldt. As far as we can surmise there may be no survivors."

Balisarius looked towards the door. His face turned to a scowl. "Survivors? No, there will be no survivors. She would have seen to that."

The attaché gave him a puzzled look. "She? Sire?" Balisarius looked back to the attaché for a moment before turning on his heels and whipping his cape to the side. He walked quickly towards the doors that became brighter the closer he was to them. Two guards opened the doors for him. He stepped onto a balcony that overlooked hundreds of thousands of uniformed Imperial troops. He raised his hand and cheers erupted from below. In front of the troops were more men in head-to-toe armor. He took in a deep breath as he scanned the crowd. They began to chant,

"Regent! Regent! Regent!"

He raised his other arm. In that moment, flower petals descended around him, falling to his feet. The parade of weapons and soldiers continued below, creating a frenzy in the troops. His eyes raised towards the sky, where a thousand Dreadnoughts hovered in perfect battle formation. He smiled and said under his breath, "There is only one of you, Arthelais, and so many more of us. Prepare to be hunted."

END OF PART 2

ACKNOWLEDGMENTS

I would like to acknowledge Zack Snyder for creating an incredible story and remaining so fiercely dedicated to such a fantastic project; Adam Forman who was insanely helpful with the nuts and bolts in the story; the ENTIRE crew at Titan Books who work so very hard to bring stories to life for millions of people; and Daquan Cadogan and Michael Beale for their tireless work on this project and believing in me all the way. A good book is a sum of all the people involved from start to finish. Editors are an essential part of the process.

Thank you to the ancestors who guide me every day.

ABOUT THE AUTHOR

V. CASTRO is a Mexican-American writer from San Antonio, Texas, now residing in the UK. As a full-time mother she dedicates her time to her family and writing Latinx narratives in horror, speculative fiction, and science fiction. Her most recent releases include *The Haunting of Alejandra* from Del Ray and Titan Books, *The Queen of the Cicadas* from Flame Tree Press and *Goddess of Filth* from Creature Publishing.

Connect with Violet via Instagram and X @vlatinalondon or vcastrostories.com